SISTER
WOLF

ANN ARENSBERG

SISTER WOLF

A NOVEL

ALFRED A. KNOPF NEW YORK 1980

THIS IS A BORZOI BOOK
PUBLISHED BY ALFRED A. KNOPF, INC.

Grateful acknowledgment is made to E. P. Dutton and
J. M. Dent & Sons Ltd. for permission to reprint an excerpt from
The Little Flowers of Saint Francis, translated by T. Okey.
An Everyman's Library Edition. Reprinted by permission of the
publisher in the United States, E. P. Dutton, and by permission of
J. M. Dent & Sons Ltd., London.

Library of Congress Cataloging in Publication Data
Arensberg, Ann [date]
    Sister Wolf.
    I. Title.
PZ4.A6797Si   [PS3551.R398]   813'.54   80-7659
ISBN 0-394-51021-6

Manufactured in the United States of America
First Edition

For Dick Grossman,

Laurie Colwin,

and

Paula Dunaway Schwartz

SISTER
WOLF

So St. Francis spoke again: "Brother Wolf, since you are willing to make and keep this peace pact, I promise you that I will have the people of this town give you food every day as long as you live, so that you will never again suffer from hunger, for I know that whatever evil you have been doing was done because of the urge of hunger. But, my Brother Wolf, since I am obtaining such a favor for you, I want you to promise me that you will never hurt any animal or man. Will you promise me that?"

The wolf gave a clear sign, by nodding its head, that it promised to do what the Saint asked.

And St. Francis said: "Brother Wolf, I want you to give me a pledge so that I can confidently believe what you promise."

And as St. Francis held out his hand to receive the pledge, the wolf also raised its front paw and meekly and gently put it in St. Francis' hand as a sign that it was giving its pledge.

Then St. Francis said: "Brother Wolf, I order you, in the name of the Lord Jesus Christ, to come with me now, without fear, into the town to make this peace pact in the name of the Lord."

And the wolf immediately began to walk along beside St. Francis, just like a very gentle lamb.

—The Little Flowers of St. Francis

Everything looks worse in black and white.

—Paul Simon, "Kodachrome"

ONE

BETWEEN EIGHT AND NINE on a June night in the highest corner of the Berkshire Hills, there is still some light to see by. On nights when the wind is high and the clouds are racing, the light in the sky is an unstable tinge, reading white, gray, gray-green, yellow-green, and smoke-yellow. By the gray-green rays Marit Deym prowled the hallway of the story under the eaves, using the turret window at one end of the corridor as a lookout for the closed van that should have pulled into the driveway an hour before. The van was coming from the Dangerfield Zoo, an easy trip on the interstate highway, but Marit had instructed the driver to take the long route on unnumbered back roads. If the van had left Dangerfield at six-thirty, there was no chance that it would meet the police patrol car, which made its scheduled rounds at eleven o'clock.

Two events wizened Marit's soul and shrank her backbone: getting through the hours from dusk to dawn, and waiting for anyone or anything. If she had been driving the van herself, her anxiety would have been manageable. As her restlessness increased, her hearing became painfully acute. Sounds from the basement earlier in the evening had not been astral miners hacking their way to free air, just the shifting and settling of the woodpile. After exploring the cellar she had gone back to the piano bench, beating sticky cobwebs out of her hair. She laid her hands on the keys and her ears began to ring. She played a page of Clementi. It was her head thrumming, not the instrument. She pitted her mind against the sound. It was a high cheeping, concerted, then intermittent, like extraterrestrials bent on reaching her from their airship. She stood up and began to follow it. Was she moving of her own volition, or half-enthralled? The blips grew louder as she reached the third floor. As she mounted the attic stairs, they rose to a manic tweeting.

The attic was a fiasco. Off a hall barely three feet wide were five rooms the size of monks' cells, impossible for storing furniture and too small for persons of conscience to sleep their housemaids. Marit inched down the hall, shoulders drawn forward, placing one foot directly in front of the other. Past the third cell, which had been fitted for a bathroom, she craned her ears. The noise was concentrated in the next room, and grew erratic at her approach. All the light switches were outside the rooms. Marit flicked the switch, but paused before the door. The cheeping stopped, its faint vibration dying in the air. Marit's breath came with a rattle in it. She threw the door wide open, so that it banged against the wall, and crossed the threshold.

The floor was speckled with discrete pellets like chocolate shot. Marit breathed better—the leavings of squirrels or house mice? Across the room, one diamond-shaped pane was broken in half. She heard rustling, and took another step inside. Up above, in a corner of the ceiling, hung many bunches of reddish-brown bats. Insulted by the light, they clustered for comfort, folding their wings, their tiny faces puckered by pique or woe. They looked foolish and defenseless, like children who put their hands over their eyes to hide, thinking that they can't be seen because they cannot see. Marit's heart hardened. They were dropping filth at a dire rate, and she was not a compost-hound. She saw a bedlamite vision of her evenings alone, gusts of bat guano swirling through the house, and that frantic chirping harrowing thoughts and sleep. But how could she herd them, one by one, out that small triangle of broken pane? How had they managed to get in? Their wingspread was nearly a foot. Were they able to crawl? For fleas, rats, and roaches she had called in Berkshire Pest. Fleas were nearly invisible; rats ate their bane and went outside in search of water; roaches expired in the woodwork, drying up odorlessly. Bats had more and stranger life to kill. The exterminator might pump in cyanide, as he had for the hornets in the loose stonework over the kitchen door. But then Marit would find a hundred little larval bodies staining the cell floor. They would start to rot in their death chamber before she could face carting them away. Perhaps the exterminator could net the bats; perhaps he could tranquilize them. She closed the door but left the light burning; it might force them out.

Marit stood by the turret window and scanned the night horizon. She looked down. The road was dark, and the driveway was still empty. She was calm now, and lucid enough to feel shame. Poor reviled bats, paralyzed in their sheaves, about as feral as motorized ducks at a boardwalk shooting gallery. She had recoiled at their dirt, having heard that they spread disease. What had stopped her from taking a club to them, since she had also been told that they bit veins and dove for women's hair? She gave herself no marks for enlightenment; clubbing and recoiling were just degrees of a killer's blow. The only crime of bats is that they hate the light and love the dark: they flout our deepest metaphor for good and evil.

Two headlight beams lit up the gravel drive. Marit drew back. The vehicle was black, but not as large as the Dangerfield van. As it inched around the drive, with minimal crunching, she made out "Sheriff, Hart County," lettered on the side of the door. It was nine o'clock, so this was not the night patrol car. The driver of the car wore a big hat. Sheriff Stoeber had the soul of a file clerk, but he dressed for business like a Texas lawman. The black sedan drove back out the way it had come in. The Sheriff might have used the driveway to make a U-turn; but it was more likely that he was watching her house for his own reasons.

In order to rile the Sheriff, she called him "Mister." "Sheriff" meant too much to a man with fat buttocks and a woman's waist. Marit was an unconscious mimic, and more than once had checked her voice as it raced up the scale to match his reedy lilt. Mister Stoeber had been her enemy since she was twelve, when he had caught her beagle dog, Snap, straying up the road and taken him to the pound, even though he was wearing a collar and a tag and Stoeber knew perfectly well whose dog he was. Her father had brought Snap back, but the dog cringed and hid, and would not eat his food the first day, or the next. When Marit petted him, he yelped and showed his teeth. There was a place on his flank, near the tail, that he would not let her touch for several months. Marit began to imagine ways of torturing the Sheriff, like coating the inside of his hat with runny cat feces, or laying a honey trail over his bedclothes and setting red ants on it. She got her chance the next summer, while the Sheriff was inside the house with her mother, collecting a pledge for the hospital. Marit spiked his gas tank with a quart of Kentucky bourbon, but she was caught in the act and spanked like a child, right in front of him.

Her parents were pleased with the Sheriff and his fawning manners. They were Hungarian aristocrats, who expected a degree of subservience, and classified the Sheriff as one of the help, someone vaguely superior in function to their butler. They thought of the selectman and the fire chief in similar fashion. Luba Deym mailed them tips from New York at Christmas, in the same amount as the checks she wrote out for the doorman and the superintendent who worked in her apartment building. Marit was growing up in America, which is a democracy, and her parents were leaving her a legacy of resentment. The Sheriff was a little man, one of the hairless meek, but he would hold her accountable for her parents' conduct. She despised him; but he had the power to thwart her. She started to watch him, like a foreign ambassador stationed in a banana republic who knows that the violence of the coming revolution will be in proportion to the harshness of the ruling dictator.

One Thursday evening in February, Marit had stood up to address the Niles Town Council. There was fog on the roads and a fine sleet beginning to fall, and the seats in the old Grange Hall were two-thirds empty. Only elders and regulars attended, who lived within walking distance of the Grange. Marit knew that the Sheriff was not expected. He had been called to Lowell that morning for a statewide police briefing on crowd and riot control. Marit had placed a stack of printed broadsides on a table by the entrance. The sheets were printed, not mimeographed, and all hand signed, so that each villager would feel that he had been personally informed of her plans and could take part in the question period afterward. Marit's address was a courtesy. She was not obliged, except by diplomacy, to ask for the villagers' approval, but her nerves were as tight as a lute, anticipating their objections. A feudal current ran deep in her character: she was in a position of power, and it gnawed her alive to underplay it. In better times, mewling and protest had been handled by edict or corporal punishment. When her father, Vladimir Deym, died, he had left fifteen hundred acres to her mother. Three years later, Luba Deym had followed him, making Marit, at the age of twenty-six, the senior landholder in Hart County.

The Deyms were Magyars. Under Duke Géza their dwelling was a hut. For nine hundred years they had worked to bury the crude stone hut. By 1915, when Vlado, aged twenty-five, and his father, the patriarch Arpàd, were driven into exile for refusing to march to war with Germans, they left behind a pile of masonry that had been known since the Renaissance as "the unfinished castle." It was also known as the castle of towers. Each generation of Deyms had building fever, and when they ran out of lateral space they aimed for the sky. The history of art and alien occupations could be read in those towers: the Fire Tower, with its Gothic spire and set of Norman bells; the minaret, a sop to Turkish rule; the Prince's Tower (in the Baroque style, to please the Austrian Hapsburgs), which housed an iron throne for visiting kings. Blocks of Carpathian granite sprawled on the riverbank. They were carried on barges down the Bodrog, on standing order, lest any Deym run out of stone and develop feelings of frustration. Like Pharaohs, they kept swarms of slaves to carry out their enterprises. Kossuth freed Hungary's serfs in 1848. Great-Grandfather Mátyás Deym did not relinquish his bondsmen until forty years later, and only then under pressure of a wheat famine, for he was in the middle of building a hunting box, with plans he had copied from Ludwig of Bavaria.

Marit took joy in her father's lineage and his childhood. His memories were as vivid as ghost stories told by firelight. His nurse, Bükki, suffered in her joints. Vlado went daily to a mineral spring in the pine grove to fetch her a cup of the sulfurous water, which she would drink, cursing and stamping and patting his head at the same time. He lingered one day, popping the sluggish bubbles in the spring's mud matrix, and saw a white knobby shape emerging on the surface. He forgot his clean blouse and put his hand in after it, pulling up one muddy bone after another, curved stalks like ribs, cranial plates, a femur as long as he was tall. It was the skeleton of a prehistoric lion, the first acquisition of the little museum he set up in the nursery schoolroom. His second find was a slim glass phial, imprinted with a rainbow. ("Glass turns iridescent underground," he explained to Marit. "Then why not people?" his daughter retorted.) Romans in passage had left the phial behind; it was unchipped, and belonged to the consular period. As she grew older, Marit had questioned the attributions, wanting to know if her grandfather had kept tame paleontologists and archaeologists, the way other noblemen kept stablehands and stewards. Then she begged Vlado to tell about the west-wing laundry floor collapsing, and the caves that ran underneath it, all the way to Czechoslovakia, and the awful ruddy stalactite formation that was afterward named "the Butcher's Shop."

The Deyms had lived in one place for nine centuries. Until 1920, not one acre of their land had been sold. The Royal Stud was pastured on Deym fields. Flocks of mouflon sheep stood the crags of the limestone foothills. Boar occupied the forests of oak, living on acorns. Deym skies still harbored the windhover, and the rare red-footed falcon. Deyms were lovers of animals, domestic or untamed. Count Lajos, who shared a birthday with Louis XV, kept a private menagerie, paying the highest sums for specimens of the cat family, snow and hunting leopards from Tibet and western India, a white tiger netted in Persia, and the broad-tailed Chinese manul. The first keeper of the cats, according to the story, was a serf whom Lajos had won in a border war. One morning Lajos saw him take a whip to the panther. He ordered the serf to be slaughtered like a fattened steer, and fed the cuts from his body to the panther and his mate. The Austro-Hungarian emperor, a follower of Voltaire, had enacted a law that gave the right of trial to serfs; but on his own lands Lajos was above the laws of the empire.

By royal decree, the Deyms were the custodians of the left hand of St. Stephen, bearing all its rings, encased in a gold hand-reliquary and displayed, behind bars, in the family chapel. To gain sanction for their whims or their ambitions, the Deyms had appealed to no one but their king. Now Marit, the last of their line, stood in the Niles Grange

Hall petitioning a group that she did not recognize as her equals. Her plan for establishing a wildlife sanctuary on her property was not a venal whim like another of her ancestors' request for exemption from the grain tithe; it was her life's work, her vocation, and her fate.

Marit had begun her speech by reviewing the list of animals that had inhabited the Berkshires only fifty years earlier, species that had been killed down to numbers that she counted off on her fingers. As she spoke, she stuttered over her notes, dropping a card or two, the cards for the lynx and the black bear, by no accident. In order to stifle alarm, she grew as sugary as she dared, pleading at length for the smaller, winsome animals—the snowshoe hare, the beaver, the silver fox. She described her negotiations with the Department of the Interior, and held up the papers, in a stiff green binder, that were her license to make her land into a private refuge for disappearing wildlife. She read a letter from Dr. Bouris, chairman of the Council of Massachusetts Colleges, praising her efforts on behalf of zoological research. She droned the letter, so that the notion of carnivores in the neighborhood should be as soporific as a bedtime tale, even to chicken farmers. Marit used other tactics: the worried diffident little frown she had worn throughout the speech; her hands that trembled and knocked over the water glass, that gripped the podium, ostentatiously, to keep from shaking. Between her purpose and these lumpish humans who might obstruct it, she raised an opaque scrim of personality, the image of a person who is desperately shy and whose nightmare is any form of public speaking. She could see her strategy working. They were transfixed, each one, by her nervousness, and barely followed the meaning of her words, the way a theatre audi-

ence is hypnotized by an understudy who may miss an entrance, drop a cue, or trip on his sword.

The people of Niles were filing back out into the foggy
night. Marit had pressed the last broadside into the last
hand, and thanked the last good soul for braving the ele-
ments. She wanted to leave the hall in order, so she set
about straightening chairs, collecting ashtrays, and turning
off lights. The light-switches were all on one board, in the
anteroom. She dimmed out the entire hall, except for the
stage lights, then threw the wrong switch, and the lobby
went dark instead. As she flicked back the lights, she heard
a low cough. She yelped, and wheeled around toward the
noise. Sheriff Stoeber stood facing her, hat in hand. By his
little smile she knew that her squeal had given him the
advantage.

"We may have to appeal, Miss Deym," he said, pulling
a sad face. "The Interior never asked the county about that
license."

"You have the right, Sheriff Stoeber," she answered,
and hugged the green binder. She was so startled that she
had forgotten to call him "Mister."

Marit pulled a chair over to the turret window. The Dangerfield van was two hours late and she was tired of standing.
The Sheriff had not come back, but the patrol car would
pass her house in forty minutes. She shifted in the chair,
which had a broken back and a wobbly leg.

The Sheriff was not her only adversary. She had as
much to fear from Commander Enos, the chairman of the
board of the Meyerling Community for the Unsighted,
which bordered Marit's estate on its eastern flank. Com-

mander Enos had God on his side. He had been an officer in the Salvation Army, and kept the title after his retirement. The Commander was tall and gray, with seven strands of hair. His limbs and parts were so attenuated that he seemed to float. His bones did not join and lock, as in mortal vertebrates; the Divine Will held his skeleton inside his skin, instead of joints. His arms seemed to be the normal length for his unusual height, but outstretched, their span was as startling as a condor's wings. Marit was a trustee of the Meyerling Community, and she dreaded functions where she might have to shake his hand: the Donors' and Patrons' cocktail party; the graduation exercises; the opening of the bakery, where the blind inmates displayed lopsided loaves and misshapen cookies. After meeting him for the first time, she had drawn her hand away and found her black glove coated with pallid scales. The Commander's skin flaked and peeled, unlubricated by animal juices; his flesh seemed to be effecting its own disembodiment. Marit called him the Holy Eunuch.

The Holy Eunuch regarded his trusteeship as a sacred mission. He proclaimed that the afflicted were made more nearly in God's image than the whole and sound, and that the care of the maimed and defective must be an act of faith, as it was in some primitive or ancient tribes where the citizens worked only for their priests, to keep them in marble palaces and linen robes and fed on rare foods. Addressing the board of trustees, the Commander would hold up both hands, thin fingers splayed, narrow fingertips as transparent as the fingertips of virgins and nuns, and implore Heaven, or some crack on the boardroom ceiling, if he, if any of them, were worthy of serving the blind.

Bishop Meyerling had left the Community an endowment so rich that it would need no supplement until the year 2000. Yet money flooded in, unsolicited, from children's allowances, widows' mites, overstocked trust funds, and guilty profits, even though Meyerling was a private school and nearly all of its pupils came from wealthy families. For the few teaching positions that opened up each year, so many applications were received that extra staff had to be hired to answer and process them. Nothing attracts financial support like a little child. In South America every female beggar walks her rounds with a baby, drugged to look sickly. When poliomyelitis was epidemic, an adult victim would not have made good poster art. The unsighted of the Meyerling Community, who inspired such generous giving, were all children, as young as five and as old as nineteen. These tender gobbets roamed loose and unguarded, learning to function without a dog or cane. If they wandered onto the Deym preserve by accident, they could not see a bear or lynx, and might be stunned or gouged by the threatened animal, perhaps to death. These children of night and pathos endangered Marit's animals. When he learned of her plans, Enos would arm the villagers with guns and torches, and march on Marit as if she were Frankenstein and the woods were alive with her created monsters. It was fortunate that the Commander did not live at Meyerling. He spent his summers at a clinic in Austria, taking injections of a serum made from the organs of sheep, which were thought to reverse the hardening of body tissues.

A horn blared as if it were stuck. Joe Miller brought the Dangerfield van in, honking like a G.I. jeep entering Paris on V-E Day. Marit made it down three flights of stairs in record time.

"Cut it out, Joe! I told you no horn and no lights!"

"You did," said Joe, jumping down from the driver's seat, "but I got to thinking what a kick if people knew what I had in here."

"I'm going to do worse than kick you," said Marit. She was fond of Joe, with his freckled, tufted head. He was the first keeper at the model zoo in Dangerfield, fifty miles over the New York border. Joe had calculated how many animals her thousand-acre refuge could support, and worked out the ratio of deer to the larger predators. He knew about the balance of nature, and the difference between summer and winter territories. He had taught her to stock the sanctuary with rabbits, mice, and moles, and to let swarms of bees loose, which would pollinate fruit-bearing trees and bushes, and make honey treats for the black bears.

"Climb right back in," said Marit, heading for the passenger's side. "We take the next dirt road up on the left. We'll let them out when we're inside the gate."

"No, I will," said Joe. "They know me."

Once they were off the asphalt and bumping down the newly cut dirt road, Marit remembered the anxiety of waiting.

"You took your own goddamned time getting here." She turned to look at him. "What accounts for the hip boots?"

"The jaguar," said Joe. "We saved the baby, anyhow. There was a lot of blood."

Hawthorn trees grew thick by the road. Their thorny branches arched over the road, clattering on the top of the van like a drumroll. The bright headlamps probed far down the tunnel of trees and across the field, and lit up a high steel gate rigged with a megaphone, which could broadcast an alarm that sounded like a fire siren.

Marit got out to unlock the gate, dismantling the alarm with another, smaller key. Joe ordered her to stay behind, and to close the gate once he got through. He handed her a long aluminum flashlight.

"Shine it on the back end of the van," he called. "I have one too, but I need more light."

Marit trained the beam. The van was lined up parallel to the gate. She saw Joe press down, very carefully, on the handle of the right-hand panel of the door, then pull the door back suddenly and spring quickly into position behind it. Marit's flashlight made a circle of light on the ground underneath the open end. Nothing happened for the space of many seconds.

Then, one after another, in a recurring arc, like trained divers, five wolves jumped into the pool of light, moving, when they landed, to the edge of the pool, into shadow. They jumped in order of their precedence in the pack. Big Swan, the father, and Lakona, the pregnant mother. George, the lame uncle, his coat matted with a yellow salve. The two young wolves, a male and a female, born in the zoo eleven months before.

In the Dangerfield Zoo, the wolves had lived in a fine cage, in a spacious lair made out of rock, like a cave. They had climbed on stone ledges, graded in size, which descended from the cave down to a gully in front of the spectators' railing. Down the ledges ran a thin stream of water, which provided drink and kept the cage clean. In the Northwest Territories, trailing caribou and elk, the wolves used to travel fifty miles in a day. Their narrow flanks were built for speed. In full cry, they have been clocked at thirty-five miles per hour. In their cage in Dangerfield they huddled like immigrants in a refugee camp who may wait many years for acceptance in their new country. Swan grew fat, and weighed a hundred and sixty pounds. Old George developed mange scabs, which no medicine had cured. From boredom, not adjustment to captivity, Swan and Lakona had mated and bred two live wolf pups. For a while the pups were taken away from Lakona. She had been grooming them compulsively, licking and nipping until there were raw spots on their skin. The wolves slept most of the day, although visitors tried to tease them into action. Young girls would cling to their boyfriends' arms, begging them not to get close to the cage, while the brave swains bayed and barked at the indolent animals.

One day Marit had walked, on an impulse, into the office of Harrison Feitler, the zoo's director, who had encouraged her to make her land into a wildlife refuge, and had offered her the zoo's resources to help her start it. Feitler had just put down the telephone. The wolves in their atrophy haunted him. He was trying to work out an exchange with Basel, the cageless zoo, but Basel was more interested in the white Siberian wolf than in the North American gray wolf. Forthwith and outright, Feitler had given his wolves to Marit, warning her only of their hostility to the lynx.

Now, as she watched them in the beam of her flashlight, shivering and uncertain, she knew how far their wildness had been compromised. Was she a stouter guardian than the iron bars of their cage? She had rescued them from humiliation, but she could not guarantee their safety. She had put up a fence, but the fence might be too low, or the lock too easy. The zoo had a squad of keepers; she was the only warden of her preserve. In order to protect the wolves, she must harbor them in secret. She had already lied to the Wildlife Registrar by omitting any mention of them in the list of animals that her land would shelter.

Marit was used to keeping secrets. She guarded herself closely, since she did not like people well enough to give them any rope to hang her. Wolves are the most important northern predator upon the larger mammals; people are the only predators of wolves. In the zoo the wolves were prisoners; behind bars they could be mistaken for big lazy dogs. Roaming unlicensed on her estate, they would be outlaws. They already had a legendary criminal record. Every right-thinking person knew that wolves attacked homesteads, ravaged herds, relished a child as much as a calf, cheated the hunter out of his yearly kill, loomed against the moonlight with red eyes and rabid jaws. They looked the part, with their deep chests and tapering skulls, and evil self-sharpening flesh teeth. The power of their bite was supernormal; they could leap on the rump of a bull moose and tear to a depth of four inches through the finely packed hair and hide. In fact, they were shy and private; they mated for life and stayed in a jealous family circle. They were as frail as Marit—even frailer, for they pulled hatred the way magnets pull metal filings.

Marit loved wolves more than any other animal, because they were the most reclusive and least valued. They tallied with her image of herself, but she did not try to scale them to her size. They were creatures and she was human, and she cherished the difference more than any likeness. When she was close to the wolves, she would learn what they could teach her: loyalty, endurance, stoicism, and courage, the traits that made them symbols of survival.

She heard a thump and saw Joe leaning into the van. He took out a burlap sack and threw it into the woods. It was full of mice, and the bag was soaked with meat blood. The elder wolves regrouped and consulted in low growls. Swan took off after the lure, but the young wolves balked and whimpered until Lakona nudged them rudely from behind.

Joe shut the doors and locked the back end of the van. "They've gone," he called. "They'll be safe now."

Marit shook her head, but he could not see her. The van backed out and she fastened the gate behind it. She said nothing to Joe on the ride back to the house, and he knew her well enough to respect her silence.

TWO

FOR A SHORT PERIOD in the early nineteen-thirties, Niles, Massachusetts, was as fashionable a resort for New Yorkers as Bar Harbor or Fishers Island. Under the glass of history, this period would be reckoned as a hiccup, or the blinking of an eye. It took the new summer gentry about five years to lose patience with the rain, bad roads, and midges, the tranquility, the grandeur of the hills, and the lack of water sports.

One of these burned-out vacationers, a banker who was related to the horse-breeding Belmonts on his mother's side, sold his new cottage as soon as it was built, before the lawns were seeded or the gutters were hung. Luba Deym did not like the country, but Vlado was coughing and his nerves were poor, and the banker's house had many Gothic details, vaulted ceilings, a crenellated roof, and four pointed watchtowers. Seen from the front, the miniature battlements were a pattern of alternating rose and blue-gray bricks. The view from the battlements reminded Vladimir of Hungary because he could not see another human dwelling in any direction.

While the painters were changing the walls from oyster to ivory, Luba began to make lists of guests for weekend parties. Her first house party, held in the second month of their residence, was also her last. Vlado did not come downstairs to greet the Nelson Cuttings or the Princess Rakoczi, who brought a gap-toothed young Englishman as her escort. He did not leave his room on Saturday or Sunday, except to pick a book from the library or to serve himself from the sideboard at mealtimes. Wearing striped pajamas, bleached and ragged, he heaped up his plate, taking time to ponder his selections, padding around the buffet in his backless leather slippers, tasting some of the dishes with his fingers, and wiping his hand on the front of his pajama jacket. He took a glass from the place that had been laid for him at the table, and went upstairs to bed, where dabs of creamed veal or spinach puree found their way onto the sheets, angering the maid, who had permission to change his bed linen only once a week. Luba took her defeat with bad grace, but she gave up importing guests from the city, and tried to make do with the company at hand, patrician but more solitary folk, who withheld their acceptance of the Deyms until their second summer in Niles. Bishop Meyerling became their particular friend, and Mrs. Paul Gilliam, the publisher's wife, who had been widowed by an idling tractor which slipped into reverse while her husband was working behind it.

When Marit was orphaned, she discovered her true social nature. Without Luba to hector and groom her, she fell
into her father's habits. She wore old clothes, stopped answering letters, and did not entertain. She pensioned off the
butler and the housekeeper, and kept Mrs. Mayo, from the
village, who cleaned the house twice a week and left a light
supper in the oven. Because she was Luba's daughter, Marit
upheld her position. She attended civic functions, but only
for groups of which she was a benefactor—the library, the
hospital, the Meyerling Community, the historical society,
and the woman's industries—trading public patronage
against the round of golf-club dances, bridge luncheons,
and little dinners. As a social being, Marit was incompetent.
She could not defer and she did not listen. If she was not
drawn to a person at first introduction, she blanked him out.
In her opinion most people were not well made and talked
too slowly. Her manner was formal or caustic, and she
made few friends. She did not need more than one person of
either sex to share her life. She had not yet found the man;
but she recognized Lola Brevard the moment she met her.
Marit and Lola had met at a Meyerling prize-day tea,
sneaked away from the ceremonies early and rudely, and
stayed up talking all evening and through the night.

Mrs. Paul Gilliam was a native of Virginia. She had known
Lola Brevard's mother since girlhood, and they had grown
up to be each other's bridesmaids. When she wanted to
engage a social secretary, she thought of Mary Brevard's
daughter. It was a nice job for a nice girl, and it left Lola
free on Saturday afternoons, which she reserved for Marit.
The sun was hot for the second week of June, so the two

friends hosed down the lawn chairs and brought a pitcher
of ginger ale and grape juice out to the terrace. At the
moment, the ice was melting and watering down the mix-
ture in their glasses. Marit stood at the parapet and pointed
her binoculars toward the meadow by the sanctuary gate,
moving the instrument up the meadow and toward the
woods, at the entrance of which was a grove of white paper
birches.

Lola was watching a bobtail cat stalking the peonies.
The cat was a gypsy, not a stray, one of the barn cats from
Jullian's dairy farm, more than five miles away. He emerged
from the bushes carrying a chipmunk by the neck. He
dropped it and started to bat at it, leaping from side to side
and pretending to pounce. Released from the monster's
mouth, the chipmunk played dead. By this time the cat was
sitting back on his haunches. The chipmunk rose up on his
two hind feet and did a dance step. Then he lifted his leg as
if he were squirting or spraying.

"Get over here, Marit," called Lola. "They're playing a
little death game."

Marit kept her binoculars trained on the birch grove.
She turned the dial that adjusts the focus, and got down on
her knees so that the railing could support her elbows.

The cat had opened the chipmunk's stomach, and sat
washing his paws while it cooled. Lola walked over to Marit,
scolding her as she went.

"You've got no business to be squeamish. What kind of
nature person acts so squeamish?"

Marit did not address the question. She raised her hind
end and leaned farther over the parapet.

"I don't want any pious anarchic goddamned back-
packers on my property."

Lola grabbed the field glasses and moved them over the meadow.

"Where, darlin'?" She rubbed her eyes. "I swear I just see worse through these things."

"Fling that riot of curls off your forehead and you might see better. There. That red spot."

Lola pushed back her bangs and tried again. This time she succeeded.

"My, he's puny. Why carry on about him?"

"They report the wild animals," said Marit. "They want bunnies and bluebirds."

"I thought you told me big animals didn't go by the fence because it's out in the open."

"This is not a state park. I won't have it. I'm going to do some reporting of my own."

Marit made a move to recapture the binoculars, but Lola kept on spying. The figure below sat down and leaned against a birch, one leg extended and one knee cocked, a poet in repose.

"Gorgeous head," said Lola, "like a falcon. He just might convert me."

"Give me those, you Tidewater sapphic." Marit raised the glasses and took another look. "Lord, you're right. He's what we used to call 'cute.' I was too mad to notice."

Lola fanned her face with her hand and pinned her hair in a knot on the top of her head. Before she settled herself in her chair, she inspected the scene of the carnage. There was nothing left of the chipmunk but the tail, the ears, and a wet patch. The cat was rolling on the flagstones, having a dust bath. Lola sat down and began to rub baby oil on her face. Drops of oil kept landing on her sunglasses. She hiked her skirt up to the middle of her thighs, and pulled her blouse down to bare her shoulders. She closed her eyes and waved a hand at Marit.

"Keep an eye on your watch for me, honey; don't let me go to sleep."

"Why?" asked Marit, who had brought her chair to the full upright position, since lazing in the sun was not one of her talents. "Does that silly woman want you to sharpen the bridge pencils?"

"Rest it, Marit; it's too hot."

"You should quit. Your brain is going to turn to cottage cheese."

Lola wiped her sunglasses on her skirt. "Don't fuss at me, angel. We've had this conversation."

"Oh, I do recall. The one about how soothing it is to live in an orderly universe. By which you meant that Mrs. Gilliam has lots of servants."

Lola did not intend to swallow this remark. She brought up a topic which she knew would be inflammatory.

"We're meeting about the cotillion. I believe I mentioned it?"

Niles Village, incorporated in 1747, had survived without a débutante cotillion for two hundred and eleven years. Lola had plotted the framework for the first Berkshire Ball, to be held on the Labor Day weekend, and for the decades of cotillions to come. Mrs. Gilliam had agreed to be the sponsor. Marit struggled with her temper for a moment, watching the bait dangling out in front of her. The bait was juicy, and she swallowed the hook. She pulled a cigarette out of the package in her shirt pocket. She chain-smoked when she was vexed.

"You love hiding, don't you? What you really love is fooling people. Poor dim old Mrs. Gilliam, trying to fix you up and marry you off. Who do you think you are, a double agent?"

Lola bared her teeth. "If I were a Jew, I gather you'd want it branded on my arm?"

"I expect you to recognize that you're acting like a hypocrite."

"You backwards bigot," said Lola, scraping the polish on her thumbnail. "I like dances and pretty clothes. I'm not a man, Marit. I will not wear pants and chop off my hair to suit your scruples."

Marit eased up and took a safer tack. She and Lola had a peppery friendship, which allowed for a good portion of strenuous wrangling. Most of the time she admired Lola ungrudgingly for the way she juggled her public and private lives.

"I don't approve of débutante mills. I think they are lowering."

"Pooh," said Lola, accepting Marit's peace offering. "You're just sour because Luba sent you to France instead."

The season that Lola made her bow to society she was chosen Girl of the Year. In Cathorne, Virginia, mothers of belles still took their daughters down a peg or two by reminding them of Lola Paige Brevard. "She wore an ivy wreath on her head, and you're bothering your daddy for orchids." "Lola Paige never hung by the phone all day long." "Serves you right. Lola Paige wouldn't break a date for a better bid; if she did, she surely never got caught at it!" "There's slouching *and* slouching, missy; Lola Paige stood just like a willow."

Some part of the local myth was Lola's beauty, which

was not the regular classical kind, but much more vivid. She had short blonde hair that curled like a crown of light, and coal-black eyes that needed no definition from paints or shadows. She was tall, two inches under six feet, and as flat in front as she was behind, but she rustled and floated when she moved, and she was constantly in motion. Her profile made a straight unbroken line from her forehead to the tip of her nose. Her mouth was wide and thin, but she was always talking, so its lack of symmetry went unnoticed. When she talked, she used her hands like a Latin; they fluttered around her face like mating birds.

Some part of the myth was purely tactics. Lola made her Aunt Fanchon Pickett dress all in black and be her chaperone at big dances in Cathorne and Richmond. Lola broke the rule and wore white her whole coming-out year, even before her official bow at the Seventh Regiment. She made every entrance heavily veiled, in a white mantilla that completely covered her face, foiled by Aunt Fan, in shiny black, who carried Lola's evening bag and dance card. The chaperone and the dance card were choice anachronisms, which got her equal marks for virtue among the parents and for affectation among her fellow débutantes. Neither opinion mattered to Lola; she knew that no Girl of the Year is ever well liked.

The chaperone was a dandy fake, had they but known it. Lola was wild, and Aunt Fan was the perfect cover. After the dances, Lola sent her aunt home in a hired car. Then she herded the timorous girls and swaggering boys into their cars, and led the caravan to the honky-tonks in nearby Gadsden. (She claimed she had once won an amateur strip-tease contest, and Marit believed her.) Back at home, Aunt Fan would knock on the Brevards' bedroom door. They propped themselves up on pillows and tried to read until Lola got in, no matter how late. "Our baby is sound asleep," Aunt Fan would whisper. "She could hardly stay awake to get undressed."

Fanchon Pickett, grand-niece of General George, was as false as brass and as tart as a crabapple. There was nobody she liked, and only one thing in the world that she cared about. That year Lola paid all of Fan's bridge debts (out of an allowance that had tripled when Lola was elected Valedictorian), and sent her spinster aunt off to Las Vegas, where she spent a week under the green light at the poker tables, sleeping two hours a night, waiting to retire until the Texas oilmen had packed it in.

Lola's wildness was of the coltish or tomboy variety: breaking curfew; outdrinking boys on boilermakers; driving on the wrong side of route 46; not being too careful of her skirts when she got out of cars or taught the Lindy. She had a dirty mouth, and ran an uncatalogued course in sex education, but she was as safe from scandal as Christopher Robin. It got noised around that Maddie Blanton was two months pregnant. "Isn't that just about the tackiest," sighed Lola when she heard it; and sexual experiments in their group lost all prestige, at least for that season. Boys never tried anything with Lola, not since she had kissed Tilden Chace in the ninth grade and scared him blue by asking him kindly why he never used tongues. The boys figured that she had picked up all that sexual lore somewhere, and credited her with experience, rather than a talent for library research. Her knowledge kept them from taking liberties, or mooning at her, which was the way she wanted it.

As further insurance, she went to dances with two escorts, and put to use her little old-fashioned dance card. It made a nice, competitive effect; the young men lined up between sets, signing its ivory leaves with a tiny pencil as thin as a knitting needle. During the fad for cutting in, Lola set herself apart by dancing each dance through with one partner. "Cutting in makes you all feel popular? Why, I'd feel like a sexual beanbag!" she had declared to a peevish delegation in the powder room. She had them there, and they hated her for it, but not one of them ventured to copy her. Pre-emptive was Lola's middle name. She had the edge on all those frilly, het-up bunnies, who could feel an erection through six layers of crinoline and tulle, and traded "stiff scores" at the end of an evening. What kept her head clear and her wits sharp was that she did not feel anything.

When she did feel something, it was her own power that she felt, the excitement of her power over Taylor Blackwell. Lola had promised her parents that she would stay interned the full two years at the Meade Institute, one of Virginia's first "early colleges." The fancy term annoyed Lola, since Meade had yet to send a girl to "later college"; but she had a certain interest in the journalism courses. Lola relaxed in that isolated setting like a retired general who had never lost a battle. Campaign memories were sweet and sufficient to her, and she rode bareback, let her hair grow, and refused invitations.

One weekend she had Gray House all to herself—or thought she did, until she passed Taylor Blackwell's suite. Tallie's girlhood bedroom had been moved to Gray House intact, with yellow gingham curtains and white eyelet valances run up specially, because the windows in the residence hall were longer than the windows at home. Tallie was hot with fever, and coughing into a French silk scarf. She was so weak that Lola had to hold a cup of mint tea up to her mouth while she lapped it with her pointed pink kitten's tongue. Lola stayed to warm her bare feet between her hands and pet her like a kitten; and stayed on to make her melt and sigh, and to tell her that her whole person looked like a crushed rose, and one part of her in particular. Tallie had covered her face with her baby hands, and when Lola paused at the door and looked back, her dark red hair was falling over her face and hands, which she still would not take down.

Tallie fell as lovesick as a clown, and just as mute. Lola might have been keeping a pet in her room, one of those tiny silky dogs that are easy to step on. She found Tallie curled up day and night in her armchair, or nesting on the quilt at the foot of her bed, raising her head and arching her body for petting when she heard Lola turning the doorknob. In Lola's arms, Tallie felt so limp and fine-boned that she could be snuffed out on the spot, or snapped in two. She would not press back, she would only yield and yield; she felt viscous, or fluid, to Lola. During one strong embrace, Lola pulled up her eyelids and found that her eyes had rolled back in her head, showing the whites, as if she were in a faint. After that, Lola took to marking her, anything to rouse her, raising bloodblisters by pinching her, setting bruises on her neck and thighs with her knuckles or teeth. She pulled ten long auburn hairs out of her head, from a patch that grew over her ear, working very carefully, setting her sharp nails right at the scalp. Tallie only opened her mouth, fluttered her fingers, and fell back into Lola's lap. Lola picked her up and slung her over one shoulder, like a rug. She carried her into her suite and dumped her on the bed. It took Lola no time to pack a bag and sign out. At home she told her parents that she had the grippe. She stayed away two weeks. When she got back, she heard that Taylor Blackwell had been taken out of school for good.

"Oof, that's revolting," said Marit, the first time Lola had told her the story. "The worst thing is the part about the crushed rose. *Wlagh*. I can hardly bear to look at you."

They were sitting in the back of a bus, coming home from the Regional Cat Show in Pittsfield, making a real teen-age scene. They laughed so hard that the driver chewed them out over the loudspeaker: ". . . if those two young ladies would *act* like young ladies." Best friends laugh like that, as if they owned the world, a kind of laughter that is better than sex or back-rubs, and puts heartbreaks and rude awakenings in a long perspective.

That same evening they made sandwiches in Marit's kitchen, and drank the good bourbon. They discussed a certain champion Rex kitten, and joked about turning Marit's acres into a cattery instead of a wildlife preserve. Marit got up to carve more slices of ham. She decided to ask the question that had been on her mind all evening. She kept her tone offhanded, as if she were inquiring whether Lola would like the bread spread with mustard or mayonnaise.

"I have to know. What is interesting about what two girls do without their clothes on? All that nursing and snuffling. How can you like it? A lot of flaps and folds and creases and empty spaces. Ladies are sewers."

Lola got a look on her face like Magellan rounding Patagonia. She stood at the prow of her argument, the wind in her hair, eyes narrowed to pierce the landmass. Marit stopped carving, arrested by so much intellectual rapture enlisted in the cause of lesbian sex. Was Lola implying that lesbian sex was a perfect circle? Her hand was tracing circles in the air. No beginning and no end, she was saying; it goes on and on; I am ready as soon as I am finished; she is ready as soon as she is finished. Every pore is an appetite. Men don't touch; they grab and they probe. There are only three good places on you, for a man—on your chest and between your legs. How can you like yourself if you see yourself the way a man sees you? Do you happen to know that you have two blue veins framing your cunt? Do you know when those veins have a pulse? (*Are you talking to me?* said Marit, lifting her upper lip. She looked mulish and threatened and idiotic. Lola made fun of her. *Oh, pardon me, please; I should have said your "area."*) Lola was sawing her hands back and forth, making parallel lines. Heterosexual sex was like a railroad line. You get on the tracks and there is one destination. You can even take the milk route, a long ride with a lot of station stops, but the trip is over when the man gets off.

There were depths of prudery in Marit, and this was ugly talk. She wanted to curl halfway around on herself, like a possum hiding. She wanted to drop the knife or throw a tantrum, if that would change the subject. There was no matching Lola in this mood. Why couldn't Marit hoist her own legs up on the table, inhale deeply and let the cigarette hang off her lip, and trade theory and anecdote like a professional? Lola was a master seducer, but Marit had spent her maturity avoiding seduction. Her public face was a scowl. She took seats next to children and ancients on the bus or airplane. On city streets her head was like a beacon rotating on its shaft. If she felt a presence behind her on an uncrowded block, she nipped into the nearest shop or building.

She was proud of her alertness; rape victims did not have her peripheral vision or her marginal attention.

The face she presented to her masculine peers was bristly and sarcastic. The boasters were mimicked; the pompous got punctured. Hunks and clubmen would back right off, with only their fur singed. There were times when her sharp tongue had failed her. The king of the stag line, voted Mr. Thinks He Is by his senior class, called her up one night after midnight to tell her that she had starred in one of his dreams. He was lying on the examining table in a doctor's office; she came in, dressed like a nurse, in a very short uniform. Marit cut him off, but the hand that replaced the receiver was trembling. She felt as if her soul had been stolen, like a Navajo Indian who is frightened of tourists with cameras. The incident gave proof to her budding opinion that all boys were like her caller under the skin.

Young men carry their self-esteem like novice waiters learning to balance a full tray on one bent palm. Marit threatened their poise, except in the case of Sandy Egmont, who had never learned to fake self-confidence where he had none. When Marit was twenty-two, Sandy had come to Niles to study owls, especially the little owl, because it had some degree of color vision. Sandy's own eyes were freakish; one was blue and one half-blue, half-brown. They had emptied the spare-parts bin when they made him, and had given him ears like a flying fox, along with great veined hands and feet like Michelangelo's David. Any sentiment that Marit possessed was reserved for Sandy, who had no vanity, who said "O.K.," like a child being brave, when she refused to kiss him, and kept right on asking her on owl walks, wanting her help in wording proposals for foundation grants, and making up packets of herbs for her to take when she had a cold. When they did go to bed, it was because they liked each other so much and they were both late virgins. It turned out that Sandy also had a great veined penis. "My, that's a nice one," said Marit, who was as curious as an ape, watching it. "I don't know much about this," said Sandy. "I'm the bell," said Marit, "you're supposed to be the clapper." They managed, because they had waited so long, and they had no nasty experiences to inhibit them.

By the time Sandy got his grant, which took him to a wilderness laboratory in Montana, Marit had decided that there should be more to sex than cuddling. If Sandy liked sex to be an extension of the nursery, a cozy, down-filled puff and a musical night-light, she wanted acts that were strenuous and athletic. It was not enough to nuzzle and suck and be soaped in the bath; she wanted to sweat and get worn out. At the train station she said goodbye fondly, and gave Sandy a quilted parka for winter duty. She went back on the defensive, sexually; it did not occur to her to go out and stalk her ultimate athlete.

A sweat bee looped across the terrace like a stunt pilot. It landed on Marit and sent electric charges into her bicep. She blamed Lola. She would have seen or heard him coming if Lola had not been drawling on, flourishing her hands, about junior committees, floral swags, supper menus, and whether the modified curtsy had gained acceptance over the deep curtsy. It seemed that all ten débutantes, with their knobby elbows and turned-in toes, were going to have to perform a mazurka. There would be branches of pale pink candles, and waiters in livery. The bee-sting angered Marit less than this drivel. She had refused to put herself forward, all white and hopeful, in her eighteenth year or since, to see who would choose her and who would pass her by. She would not stand like a patient white bullock while prize ribbons were attached to her harness. She hated fairy stories, except for ones in which princesses set their suitors hard tasks (taking a pearl out of a frog's belly without killing the frog), then harder tasks (running through a field sown with knife blades), then impossible ones, like climbing a sleeping giant and putting his eyes out. She would rather dry up inside her husk then lay her neck under the guillotine of male approval. Her sense of humor had abandoned her for the time being or she would have seen Lola in a comic or seditious light, pimping for herself among all those new-blown débutantes, boring through the System from within. Nothing allied her with Lola at the moment. She thought it might be nice to start a fight.

"You're like a bloated sheik with a harem. Do something useful for a change."

"Oh, you are so saintly." Lola arched her chest toward the sun. "Fixated on your animals, like my horse-crazy cousin, Pie. We heard her galloping up in her room, for hours on end. She was nearly twenty."

When Lola fought dirty, Marit gulped air. Sooner or later it made her sick to her stomach.

"I won't be on any committees. I won't even go. I may go and throw rocks through the window."

Marit had scrunched up her face and raised her fists, like a child about to fly into a pet. She looked so foolish that Lola whooped and laughed until her sunglasses bounced off her nose and into her lap.

Marit got out fast. She ran into the house and climbed

up to the battlements, out of Lola's line of vision. She had
blood in her eye. She scanned the lower meadow and the
birch grove. There was the lone male backpacker, sacked out
full-length under a tree, with one arm covering his face.
Wouldn't I like to pick him off, thought Marit; I'd give him a
scare. Her old BB gun was in the broom closet, for some
reason, and so were two fencing masks, both rusty, and one
with the wire mesh torn. BB-gun wars had been good sport
when she was twelve. She had made up teams with the
Browers, three rough boys whose father ran the hardware
store and issued the hunting and fishing licenses. The fencing masks protected their faces, and they had worn two layers of winter clothing on their bodies, in spite of the heat.
The BB shot raised blue welts right through the woolen
layers, and smarted fiercely. She was good at standing pain,
and could fight at closer range than the three boys. Her
specialty was the suicide rush. She scattered nests of Browers by barreling straight at them, making Japanese noises,
and taking fire from all three guns without falling back. The
blue welts got ulcerated. Naked, under her mother's angry
eye, Marit looked like St. Sebastian after his arrows had
been pulled out. The wars ended, the sores dried up, but
those tiny bruises had taken a year to fade away.

The backpacker rolled over on his stomach. He bent his
elbows and flexed his feet and did some pushups. Then he
picked up his canvas bag and rooted around in it. Marit
cocked her forefinger and raised her thumb, pointed the finger at the top of his head and made halfhearted shooting
sounds. He did not whirl around or clap his hand to his
head; he had no sense of danger. He got up to go. Up from
the meadow grass also rose a bird, crying a call, *kill-deer,*

kill-deer. It flew low, then skittered along the ground. Marit watched it run and rise back into the air. The killdeer was gone, the hiker was gone, and so was Marit's little fluster. She ran down the stairs to hug Lola, who was much too debonaire to hold a grudge.

THREE

GABRIEL FRANKMAN CARRIED sunflower seeds in his knapsack, and a compass and clean socks. He hiked through the woods above the Deym sanctuary in the daytime, innocent of trespass, naming and feeding the birds, who became his friends. With his bright brown eyes, beak nose, and quick hands, Gabriel was no stranger to the birds. He reached the wood by walking three miles along the highway from the Meyerling Community, where he taught during the winter and summer sessions. He had marked his own trail through the trees and bushes, although he sometimes followed the new dirt road. Gabriel strode or stomped, as his mood dictated, as far as a semicircular clearing of white birches, where he halted at the sight of the stone house on a rise across the meadow.

During the summer, Gabriel's duties at the Meyerling Community were scheduled by rotation, but it was rare that the afternoon hours from three to five did not fall free. By unspoken agreement the Meyerling teachers wrote down their destinations in the off-duty sign-out book, in case there was a crisis or an accident in their absence. Although he was as disciplined as a novice in a religious order, Gabriel did not obey this rule. It cost him something, in tenser nerves, to flaunt it. It would have cost him more to let them know his movements. He had entered a life of service, in which some margin of freedom is doubly precious, both for the renewal of vows and for the protection of the server from resentment. The blind children who came to his poetry workshops got more from him than the skills to earn their secondary diplomas. He wanted to give them the world through their imaginations. He tried to fire them with fine examples. He told them that the heroes of myth and drama were their natural kin, because their blindness was the mark of a special destiny, like the caul surrounding the head of a newborn child, which brought good fortune. They must rise to the occasion of their blindness and bend their efforts to be worthy of their gift. If Joan of Arc had not learned how to hear her voices, they would have called in vain until the battle for France was lost.

Miss Fellowes, who had been at Meyerling since its founding, sat in the back of the room at Gabriel's first class. She took him into the living room afterward for a cup of coffee. "We try to treat them like normal children," she began; but Gabriel did not accept the mild reproof. "If you pretend they are ordinary," he answered, "you will crush their spirits." During a catalogue meeting later that fall, Gabriel insisted that they drop the word "creative" from the title of his writing course. All of living is creative, he explained, not just the pockets of people who make art. Gabriel's colleagues were disturbed by his exalted way of speaking, but they were relieved when he did not criticize their methods. No one was more relieved than Henry Dufton, who liked to be called the Head Teacher, because he found the term "Headmaster" autocratic. Mr. Dufton was almost blind himself. He wanted life to be even and smooth, just as he preferred to stroll in the formal gardens where he could never trip on a root or get smacked across the face by reaching branches. More than Gabriel's unsparing work and his love for children, Mr. Dufton valued the fact that he never raised his voice.

Gabriel's gentle manner and voice did not come to him easily. He paid out his gentleness like a tithe, and his conscience exacted heavy dues. There were sins on his conscience, which he summoned up regularly and marched in review to keep him on guard against future crime and error.

When he was in the seventh grade he had won the hurdles at the track meet, taking the honors from Johnny Meara, who was a sore loser. Johnny hung around until the crowds had disappeared, watching Gabriel remove the hurdles and rake the track. He went over to Gabriel and called him a dirty name. Gabriel picked up a rock and caught him on the chest. He left Johnny lying on the empty cinder track. The wound on his chest was staining his jersey with blood.

When Gabriel got home, he was late for supper. He confessed to his parents and told them what Johnny had called him. Gabriel's mother lifted tired, frightened eyes to her husband. " 'Sheeny' means 'Jewboy,' Ava," his father answered. His parents took him out of the Catholic school, which was only a block away from his home; but for two weeks he was kept in moral quarantine. His parents did not speak to him, or meet his eyes. The family ate their meals in the kitchen by the wood stove. A plate was left for Gabriel on the glassed-in back porch, which was unheated.

Gabriel's great-great-grandfather was a Jew turned freethinker and a music teacher. He had left Hesse-Darmstadt in 1848 to avoid conscription. Once he had settled in Hobart, Indiana, he embraced his wife's faith and joined the Presbyterian church in gratitude for their safe passage to America. His great-grandson—Gabriel's father, Joel—was a trustee of the local congregation. Gabriel knew that he was being ostracized not for defending the race of his remote ancestors but for being ashamed of it. Racial shame was the least of his transgressions. He had left Johnny Meara alone, losing blood, and trying to crawl by inches. He had waited an hour before reporting the fight to the track coach. By the time Mr. Meara and the coach had reached the field, Johnny was unconscious.

Ostracism from the family circle was too light a penalty. The rest of his punishment Gabriel administered himself. Studying at the back of the homeroom while his classmates took Catechism, he had overheard Father Adrian describing the penances of holy monks and zealous retreatants. Now Gabriel pictured himself as a sore and an abscess, from which vile poisons ran; and he wrapped knotted lengths of rough packing twine around his waist to wear all day and night underneath his clothes. He closed the shutters of his room and lived in darkness, imagining the stench of the damned burning in Hell, searing his own palms

over a candle flame until he retched from the pain. In order
to simulate Johnny Meara's wound, he drove a sharp lead
pencil into his breast, but he broke the point, and only made
a bruise. A braver boy would have tried it with a penknife.
He remembered the leeches suspended in a jar at the phar-
macist's. He could get some and let his own blood, draining
off his evil temper at the same time. But he sickened at the
thought of touching the broad flat worm, and he did not
know how to remove a leech without leaving some of its
suckers in his skin.

Gabriel enrolled at Western Indiana College of Divinity
on his sixteenth birthday. Joel Frankman had used his influ-
ence to get his son a scholarship. Gabriel was young to be
entering college and small for his age. He measured five feet
five inches and weighed a hundred and thirteen pounds. He
would put on more weight, but he never grew any taller. It
was no comfort, ten years later, when his fiancée told him
that John Keats was only five feet two. He was stuck with a
runt's body, and he found out that divinity students are no
kinder than other college boys. Gabriel was so belligerent
that he brought the jeers down on his own head. The sheeny
fights were over; now "mouse meat" and "fly bait" were the
fighting words. Gabriel went right for the bruisers; he never
picked on anyone his own size. He was as battle-scarred as a
tomcat, with a torn ear, most of the time, and two black
eyes. His Homiletics professor worried about him, and arranged a meeting with the boxing coach. By then Gabriel
weighed enough to qualify in the bantamweight class. He
made the team, but he had pugnacity left over. Even the
bullies were reluctant to tangle with a star boxer, so he took
his load of anger off campus to the dives in nearby Val-
paraiso. In his senior year he messed up his hands so badly

that he could not put on gloves and was dropped from the Olympic tryouts. He could not type or write, because his hands were wrapped with yards of gauze, so he had to take his final examinations orally. Axel Crowl, who taught Church History, advised Gabriel not to go into parish work until he had mastered his own personality. Dr. Crowl was a happy old man, plump and pink-cheeked and shorter than Gabriel. He understood the yen for purity pinioned inside Gabriel's still-adolescent body, the feats of studious discipline followed by outbreaks of violence. "There are saints who were brawlers and street fighters," said Dr. Crowl, "but their way was the hardest. You must forgive yourself, Gabriel; and forgive your father for trying to teach you meekness instead of humility."

Gabriel listened to his good adviser and paid him heed, in his own way. He had a wide penitential streak, but he could turn it to positive service, instead of using it against himself. In his last term of college his inner landscape was a perpetual twilight-gray; he knew that it was time to break out and try living in the sunshine. He did not literally mean the tropics, but he copied down a notice that was thumbtacked under "Employment Opportunities" on the bulletin board outside the Dean's office. The Francis Makemie Medical Mission in Cuba, province of Pinar del Río, town of Cabo Yegua, wanted a combination orderly and driver; room and board, and seventy dollars a month.

Gabriel stayed in Cuba for five years. Very soon he moved out of the blocklike mission building and paid board to a widowed childless *guajiro*, Santiago Vélez, who lived in a palm-thatched cottage and raised a flock of chickens. Pepe's chickens were white, but scratching in the red Cuban soil had turned them rusty. The roosters stopped diving for

Gabriel's ankles after a while, and allowed him to pick up the laying hens to inspect their nests. Gabriel liked the food that Pepe cooked, *yuca* and *malanga* and other tubers mashed with rice, and sometimes ground beef spiced with raisins and green olives. Pepe helped Gabriel to learn Spanish by pointing at familiar objects—*el vaso, la cama*—or by imitating actions: a plant growing (*crecer*) was one of his best; a hen laying (*poner*) was an even richer sight.

Over at the mission *clínica* and out in the ambulance, Gabriel learned as many skills as any licensed paramedic. This was farm country and the base of the Midland Cement Company. With so much heavy machinery around, accidents in the fields and at the works were frequent and serious. Nothing seemed gruesome to Gabriel, under that sun and sky, until the night when the Midland day foreman sneaked into the clinic by the back entrance and hissed from the shadowy doorway at Gabriel, who was the only man on duty. The fingernails of his right hand had been torn out. He could barely stand, and his eyes were wild with pain or fear. He made Gabriel bandage him and shoot him with morphine right there in the doorway. A week later, Pepe told Gabriel that Mariano the foreman was safe now in the Sierra Maestra, with *Fidel y los barbudos*.

Gabriel snapped out of his almoner's daydream and took a look around him. Among the groups of blue-uniformed *guardia civil* he noticed more and more reinforcements wearing khaki. He started to count the army jeeps on the streets and back roads. Twice a week the Midland limousine stopped for Cifuentes, the chief of police, and drove him out to the company golf course. One day Gabriel was called off ambulance duty to assist the mission doctor in setting the leg of a Midland laborer. When the doctor told him he would be immobile for two months, the patient broke down completely. He would get no leave or compensation for his accident, because a handbill bearing the picture of a bearded man had been found in his overall pocket during a search of the plant workers' locker room.

Now Gabriel's vision began to alter, as if his eyesight had been damaged by a sty. Even the light changed. The sun, which had danced on the sea and sparkled off the white colonial housefronts, glared down on the town of Cabo Yegua. He saw that the Spanish grillework was rusty and corroded, and the fitted roof tiles loose and chipped. Every oleander bloom was edged with brown. Gabriel had thought of Pepe as a kind of Cuban Thoreau, who had chosen a simple, independent life. It struck him all at once that Pepe was poor, not frugal, that his chickens were scrawny, that his clothes, which were so neatly mended, were almost threadbare.

Gabriel had made some American friends, the children of executive officers of the Midland Cement Company. The young people he met went to college in the States, but they came home during every term break to go to parties, where they danced all night and spoke to each other in Spanish. The girls were not allowed to go out with Cubans, so Gabriel was invited to ease the shortage of boys. Nancy Billups gave a party over the Easter vacation, in honor of one of her college friends, Francesca Hadley. Gabriel danced the slow dances with Francesca, who was wearing flat heels and only came up to his ear. When she answered his questions, she stood on the tips of her toes to make herself heard. Her fine hair brushed his cheek and her skin smelled like vanilla. Gabriel handled her very delicately, like one of those painted eggs that have had the insides blown out of them through a pinhole. That Sunday he and Francesca rode into Campeche Valley on a pair of mules to see the *mogotes*, geological hummocks left by backwash from a receding glacier. Francesca wore a big straw hat, but she began to droop from the heat before too long. On the way back he sat her in front of him and held her up, while the riderless mule walked behind them, led by a rope that was tied to Gabriel's belt. Francesca was so pale and fair, with her slim gypsy feet and small nose, that he fell in love without asking himself permission. A month after her vacation was over, Gabriel left Cuba to its own destiny, bought an airplane ticket with his savings, and rang the doorbell of her apartment in New York.

Back in New York, like a princess in her tower, Francesca Hadley was studying the arts of Islam. Gabriel took care of her for three years, while she worked toward her doctorate and he started the poetry workshops at Duberman Elementary School which were later picked up as a model by the Manhattan public school system. Gabriel's pupils were regular rough-and-tumble kids, but Francesca was like an overbright child, the kind that educators call Exceptionally Gifted. Her scholarship was flawless, as was her mastery of Arabic, but she had no life skills.

Adorable Francesca, with her egg-yellow hair and the soft blonde down on her face. She was a comical little beast, dreaming in the kitchen, pouring milk through a frozen shrimp soup can onto the floor, because she forgot that she had opened the can at both ends. There were squirrel's nests all over the apartment: Gabriel found a bathing cap filled with orange peels on the top shelf of the china cupboard, and a trove of garters and buttons in an empty box of macaroni. Francesca was so myopic that she needed glasses to find her extra pair of glasses, which was a mercy, because she never noticed spilled coffee on the counter tops, mold in the folds of the shower curtain, or what her housemother at boarding school used to call "dust kitties" under the bed. Her method was simple: it was time to clean house when the closets and drawers were empty and every item in her wardrobe lay strewn on the sofa and chairs and the living-room rug. Gabriel found himself turning into a Scotch nanny, wagging his finger under her nose, and scolding as he picked up after her.

Airy fragile Francesca, a neutral reproof was like a tongue-lashing to her, a spark of irritation was an indictment of her whole character. "Shrink" and "cower" had been fancy metaphors to Gabriel, or something that puppies did when they wet the floor and not the newspapers. Francesca acted out both verbs when she was reprimanded, with some quailing and flinching thrown in besides. Gabriel practiced saying things like "There are eggshells in the laundry hamper" in a monotone, but her brows would knit and her mouth would start to tremble before he could finish the sentence. Living as he did under the myth of his own vile temper, he felt he was performing contortions of self-control. Still she would react as if he were a sadistic child with a toy chest full of stuffed animals to brutalize: some days she would be the rabbit whose ears he pulled off, and other days the bear whose glass eyes he extracted. He hated the image of himself that he saw in her eyes, but he bowed his neck to it. If he could get through a day, then a length of days, without making her cry, he could atone for his sins of anger and propitiate the violence within him. He saw clearly that it would be a lifelong task, so he asked her to marry him, and she said yes, with a fey, sweet smile.

He was asking too much of himself. Such marvels of therapeutic forbearance cannot be exercised in close domestic quarters. He began to wish for a neurosurgical procedure that would cut out his irritability without otherwise harming his brain. Free from criticism, Francesca thrived; she trilled and crowed and made messes like an infant, and never once caught him drumming his fingers or holding his tongue. He took no pride in his silence. Suppressing critical words was no good if he could not vanquish critical thoughts.

After months of this unnatural regime, he convinced himself that she was secure enough to let him speak and act normally again. She was a bubbly little sprite, and sprites, like cats, have many lives. He was pleased with himself, and began to relax his guard. One night he sat down to add some new exercises to his poetry workbook. The workbook was missing from his desk and from his shoulder bag. He thought he must have left it in his office at school. He went into the bathroom to wash his face. The soap slid out of his hands, onto the floor, and under the old claw-footed bathtub. On his hands and knees he reached for the soap, and saw a mustard-colored paperbound volume wedged between the tub and the bathroom wall. He pulled it loose, shredding the covers and several waterlogged pages as he did so. Francesca liked to read in the bathtub. She had so many fines for damaged books that Butler Library had cut off her borrowing privileges.

She was curled up on the sofa, eating an apple. Gabriel raised one eyebrow, in a parody of menace, and held the spongy workbook out in front of him. He might have been raising a dagger to smite her. The apple dropped out of her hand. She started to shake her head and shrink away from him. She kept opening her mouth, fishlike, trying to say "no," but terror palsied her vocal cords. He stood watching, baffled and goggle-eyed, as she inched off the sofa and toward the door. He glanced quickly over his shoulder at the mirror on the wall to see if he was wearing the shape of a fiend. He looked at the workbook, which was still a workbook, not a bludgeon or a loaded gun. She was standing in front of the door, both hands behind her back, grasping the doorknob, her breast thrust forward, heaving. It occurred to him that she was acting and, in the next instant, that it did not matter; she was so absorbed in her role that the line between pretense and belief was nonexistent. He moved a half-step toward her and she screamed like a weasel being hoisted in a snare. The ugly noise set him on fire. For the first time in three years he yelled his brains out, liberated by the injustice of her reaction. He heard his own voice thundering in his ears, drowning out the sound of the door as it slammed behind her. He kept on yelling to an empty house, until his knees buckled and he fell on the couch, light-headed and punch-drunk and spent.

The telephone woke him out of a stony sleep. An intern at the Hope-Downtown emergency room wanted him to come over and claim the body of a young blonde girl who had crossed Greenwich Avenue in the middle of traffic and been hit by a tow truck. There had been nothing to identify the victim except a frayed name tag on her underpants—sewed on by Francesca's mother when she had sent her, at age thirteen, to summer camp.

*　　*　　*

Francesca was buried in the old graveyard of All Souls in Matlock, which lay one town east of Niles Village. Earlier Hadleys had summered in Hart County. They had endowed the porch and bell tower of the church, in exchange for a bucolic resting place. Francesca's headstone was a thin marble slab carved to imitate the primitive markers that surrounded it. Very soon it began to tilt, like the older stones. Gabriel traveled to the graveyard every weekend. He took the night owl up and the milk train back, laying his sleepless nights on Francesca's grave instead of flowers. He got an offer to teach at the Meyerling Community. The location would ease the toil of visitation, but he debated, for that very reason, whether he should take it. He bargained himself into the job: while he worked at Meyerling, he would visit Francesca's grave twice a week, instead of only once, and he would walk to Matlock in any kind of weather, five miles going and five miles coming. He had been keeping her memory alive in a listless, automatic sort of way, like a bored and feverish child picking at chicken-pox scabs. He could not mourn, but he felt that he ought to. He made another bargain with himself. If he used the hike to Matlock as one focused act of grieving, like a meditation, he could have the rest of his days clear and unencumbered. Little sticky bits of Francesca's personality still clung to him, and he needed more time to work them off.

Gabriel began to hike off his liability to Francesca, and never thought of her betweentimes. He stopped hunching over and stood as straight as a recruit again, reaching for every fraction of an inch of height. He was free to think. The inside of his head was blue horizonless space, where before his thoughts had been penned in his brain like rats in an attic room. Under so much light, his own vocation began to grow. One evening he sat at his desk facing an empty yellow sheet of legal foolscap. He was expected to contribute a report to the case file of a disturbed girl student. He was poised for the task, but the Muse sometimes operates by stealth. From his pen, like automatic writing, came the First Exercise in Self-Mastery, for the book of poems that would become his life's work. For some weeks he sat down at his desk every night. He pushed well into the Third Exercise. He lived and wrote like a column of white fire. But every forward movement breeds inertia, and one day Gabriel lost his balance, in a sweat, and stumbled back to safety, as if writing poems were as dangerous as walking a tightrope across a canyon. Writing poems distracted the soul and led to selfishness. The disturbed student, Aimée Dupuis, had followed him out of the classroom, plucking at his sleeve. She wanted to tell him her nightmare, which was always the same one. He felt the plucking, but he did not hear her voice. He shook off her fingers as if he were brushing away a horsefly, and then a sound of a higher pitch reached his ears. The girl was crying, and he had made her cry.

What distinguished any pillar of fire or poet from Attila or Tamburlaine? If he placed himself at the center of the universe, little people would be maimed and overrun. There was no room in his life of service for a poet's hubris. Gabriel was in anguish. For a time he lived by shorter and shorter shrift. The Caretaker pushed the Poet down a manhole, fed him on scraps, and kept him in the dark.

Gabriel looked around for tasks that would drain his time and energy. He set up sacrifices like trip wires, in order to thwart his passage back to poetry. Where he saw need, he dove in like a sponge-diver; and there was need and pathos everywhere he looked. Children are poignant in and of themselves. Children in institutions break your heart. Blind children in institutions are sacred trusts. Gabriel's vision of these young blind was only partial. He willfully did not notice, nor could he recall, that Wyeth threw food, John stole cigarettes, and Preston had hoisted Nannie Phillips into an apple tree and run away while she was screaming to be let down. All that Gabriel saw, or would retain, was their habit of walking around with their faces lifted, as if they were holding sweet conversation with Our Lord. They were denied the world of appearances and its distractions, so they must be in closer touch with the realm of Ideas. If one of these vessels of truth and beauty should bruise its shin, Gabriel ministered to the hurt like the Magdalene anointing the feet of Christ. One day Nannie had sat at the back of his classroom, frowning. Tears flowed in a steady stream from her closed blind eyes. When the class was over, he dropped to his knees by her chair and enfolded her. He rocked her in his arms, and stroked her thick, dark hair. "What makes you cry, my poor Nannie? There is no trouble so big it can't be talked about." "For Pete's sake," said Nannie, wriggling free of him, "I've got hay fever and my eyes are watering awful."

After a number of these outbursts, the children began to avoid him. Gabriel's timing was off, and he sounded false, even to himself. His chest was tight from the press of his humane obligations. He tried to force himself to move and speak legato, but he had developed the reflexes of an intern on call, a flair for emergency which alarmed his shy charges, who were as skittish as rabbits.

One night he was putting the youngest boys to bed. They lived together in a dormitory room which held five cots. An hour after lights-out, as he made the usual bed

check, he heard Michael—he thought it was Michael—
whimpering under the covers. Dreading suffocation, menin-
gitis, burst appendix, Gabriel crossed the room in one
bound, knocking over a chair, which fell with a crack to the
floor. The whimper spread from cot to cot, until five little
boys sat rocking back and forth, fists pressed to their eyes,
mewing and moaning for a night-lamp. Gabriel's suddenness
reminded them that they had been afraid of the dark before
they lost their sight.

Gabriel stayed in the room until the last boy fell asleep.
He left one light burning when he tiptoed out. Stumbling
the first few yards down the hall, clumsy from the shame of
frightening children, he went up the stairs to his room. He
paused for a moment outside his door; then he hurried down
three flights of stairs without being seen, and left the house.

Gabriel knew his way through the Deym woods as well
as he knew the floor plan of his room. In the daytime he had
used a square of hard white chalk to blaze his route. The
chalk marks had stood up well against the rainfall. He
counted on the moonlight to pick up the marks and show
him the trail, but the blazes dimmed out at night and he
could not find them. He was not afraid, but the woods were
no longer familiar. He passed by a tree whose roots had
straddled a boulder. There were rocks in his path, so he
walked with his eyes on the ground. Damp seeped through
the soles of his shoes and the earth felt spongy, as if there
were springs running under this part of the wood. As he
walked, he let his left palm drag across the bark of a row of
pines, bark that was sharp enough to scrape but not pierce
his skin. The alley of pines led him downhill into a clearing
carpeted with moss that was as white as tundra lichen. He
tore a moist clump of moss to hold in his smarting palm, put

his face up to the moon, and closed his eyes. The warmish breeze stirred his hair and caressed his neck. Then a cold current shocked his eyes open—December air that might be sweeping down from a lunar plain. In the trees ahead he saw streaks of light, like a moonbeam running. The flash circled back beyond the right-hand edge of the clearing, and he watched it until his head could swivel no farther. He thought it might be marshfire, so he pushed on into the grove to see if he could find the bog that had sparked the lights.

The grove was so dark, after the moonlit clearing, that it made his ears ring. He felt his way forward, groping for support. Both hands fell on coarse, dry tufts. Strange vegetation, springy like fur, long enough to tangle his fingers in. Then the fur bushes, thigh-high, lurched and bumped him, penning him in tight, making snarling and whirring sounds, breaking into a trot, and driving Gabriel between them.

He made his mind as blank as the moon, which shone brighter now, as he ran in that narrow, fur-bounded channel, out of the dense grove of birches and onto the meadow. He held his head up for fear of what he might see. Once he tripped and lost his gait. He felt a nip on his ankle: in the real world no bush has teeth. He looked down to identify the biter; he saw two yellow eyes. A nip on the other ankle. They were on a countdown. They herded him back in line, jostling him from flank to flank, two doglike creatures or creaturelike dogs, with plans of their own.

When they reached the short grass, they raised a low, broken cry, whining or pleading. Above the lawn loomed a house. Someone stood at the top of the double staircase to the terrace, calling back in the same plaintive tone. They barked twice, and were answered by two barks. Gabriel had been running with his arms locked across his chest. Since the shape on the landing was human, he dropped his hands onto the back of each animal to balance him during the last sprint toward the house. Now they were his guardians, not his captors.

Gabriel knew the house from his afternoon walks. It belonged to Marit Deym, a woman close to his age, who had a private zoo. He had heard the townspeople grumbling about the animals. He had never seen the owner of the house, who was descending the outside staircase, holding up two clean white bones.

"Who are they?" asked Gabriel. He flinched, watching them lunge at the food she threw, growling and slavering as if the bones were small carcasses.

" 'Who' is good," said Marit Deym. "I could weed people out by 'who' or 'what.' " She called to one of the animals. "Swan! Take off."

The greater male, with the silver ruff, dropped the bone at his feet. The young male rolled over and lay with his paws upraised. They were sending a signal to their mistress, who knew the code and walked into their midst to scratch their ears and stomachs. She gave up scratching before they were ready, so they pulled her down with them, pinning her between their bodies and yipping for more. At one point Gabriel lost sight of her completely; she was buried under fur. Then she struggled free and clapped her hands smartly, three times. When the animals were on their feet, she shoved them forward. They loped away over the lawn and down the meadow.

"Timber wolves," thought Gabriel, but he was thinking

out loud. He moved to the bottom step and sat down hard.

"Wait here," she commanded. "I have to lock them in."

If he had entered the religious life, Gabriel would have been well suited to it. He possessed discipline and a sense of culpability, and, above all, a quick acceptance of the marvelous. During his working day, he lived on red alert; in the midst of danger, he became serene. Disastrous expectations fulfilled made him loose and languid. A pair of wolves had seized him in the woods and delivered him to their keeper, who showed no surprise. He did not ask himself if they were acting under orders, or how she knew that he was on her land. It was easier to suspend debate and doubt, to take for a fact that the fiercest predators could be tamed by a girl in a bathrobe and bare feet.

It was more comfortable to give up thinking for himself, to follow the girl across the terrace and through the French doors, to sink into the velvet cushions on the sofa, and to take a glass from her hand, although he did not drink liquor. There is a sensual release, in rigid, watchful people, that accompanies the surrender of the will. He sank back deeper into the cushions, which were a warm brown, the color of his eyes. The strange girl sat across from him in a wing chair, establishing lines of precedence, not of intimacy. One standing lamp was lit, behind her chair. The light glanced on her small straight nose and bare sharp knees. Her hair was short and cut in feathery layers. Her ears were pierced with tiny jeweled studs. The robe she wore was tied at the waist, but the sash had loosened enough to show that she wore no nightdress underneath. He had never known a slender girl with heavy breasts.

If Gabriel had chosen a life of religion, he would have

adapted without resentment to the rule of chastity. Every evening at bedtime he performed a review of the day, to monitor himself for lapses into anger. His vigilance held other physical instincts in check. He wanted to make restraint a matter of habit, like combing his hair and washing his hands before meals. Women liked him because he looked them in the face; they never caught him scanning their calves or their ankles with his eyes.

Marit Deym's face was in shadow. The lamplight modeled the triangle at the base of her neck. As she leaned forward, the folds of her robe fell open. The skin of her breast was smooth and very white. She was talking urgently, but he only heard snatches of words—sheriff, Dangerfield, license. At one point he gave her his name. She wanted him to forget that he had seen the wolves. She did not seem to notice that her robe was in disorder, unless she thought it was the surest way to get his promise. His palms began to feel alive, as if he were holding her breasts and weighing each one in his hands. She got up and moved toward the couch, tying her sash in an unconscious gesture. She had come to plead her cause at closer range, but his business with her was more serious. He held and kissed her haphazardly, a nostril, her jawbone, her clavicle, her windpipe, her chin. He could not find her mouth until she found it for him.

The next day, when he was back on red alert again, he would remember that there seemed to be two of her, two lean flannel-robed Marits pressing in on either side of him as they went upstairs. Her bed was the size of a cot, and that cot felt as big as a soccer field. He had shared a large bed with Francesca, but the covers were neat in the morning and the sheets stayed tucked in. Francesca lay very still, with her arms at her sides. When he was finished, she would get into her favorite position, nestled up against him like a squirrel, with her knees in his stomach. When he turned over on his other side, she clamped onto him from behind. Francesca did not like to be wakened or handled once she had fallen asleep. The girl who kept wolves did not let him sleep all night.

Gabriel had lived with his anger so long that he disregarded any other passion. He took for granted that anger had subsumed every troublesome impulse, weakening his sexual inclination as much as his appetite for food or luxury. His restricted experience had taught him that sex is useful for showing affection and releasing tension. He did not know, until that night with Marit, that joining with another person could make the life he was leading seem as vain and as sad as an exile's. He had been living from day to day, without hope for the future, under a judgment that he himself had drafted and imposed. In the person of this tense, shy girl he saw a higher court, which could revoke his sentence and give him back his freedom. He wanted to speak, but she seemed so replete and peaceful that he kept his counsel. She would recoil if she heard a confession from a stranger. She would think that he was deluded or dishonest, turn him out of her bed, and banish him to Meyerling, that model prison for a model prisoner. He could not speak, but his body could speak for him, so he touched her lightly, and heard her murmur in response.

Gabriel was up and gone by six o'clock, while the fields were fogbound. Marit's wits were also fogbound; it was her first white night. Every time they had come apart, Gabriel lay separate, locked in his contours like a crusader on his slab.

Didn't lovers hold on to each other after disconnecting? She
had kept quiet and cramped, for fear he might think she was
expecting it; and when acknowledgment came—a flicker of
fingers on her hip—she was startled, and made a queer
sound.

The last time, she held him and kissed him at the moment of severance, many kisses on his shoulder and the hollow of his throat. He pulled back but she pressed him down,
a sign that she welcomed his weight, that he could not hurt
her. When there was no space between them, she felt that
nothing could hurt her. This slight fine-boned man was her
creature. Now that she had found him, he could come to her
every night. Her house would be the place where he rested
and restored his forces. She would take him to the sanctuary
and acquaint him with her work. She could not lock him in
with the animals; she must let him come and go of his own
free will.

Gabriel slipped out of her arms, which had loosened
their grip. He rolled over and faced the door, with his back
to Marit. She felt the blood rise to her face, a flush of embar-
rassment. She had held him too tightly. Perhaps she had
obstructed his breathing. She was untutored in so many
points of amorous etiquette. She was a rube at love, ham-
handed and crude, and he was a gentleman. He must have acquired his grace and polish in other beds, refining his skills
until they became instinctive. How many beds and how
many partners? Which one had warned him that neither
breast should be neglected? Which one had taught him the
use of teeth and the art of tongues? She felt a sharp pain,
exactly at the center of her ribs. She dug her face into the
pillow to stifle a sudden cry.

When Gabriel rose to dress, his eyes were hard and

harried. His face had the pure, drawn look of a fallen anchorite. She had gone to bed with Pan and got up with St. Anthony the Hermit. The change in him frightened and smote her; she felt unworthy. She lay watching him put on his shirt, pulling the covers up under her nose, because her teeth were chattering. He dressed with his head down, half hidden behind the door. He yanked his belt through the buckle too tightly, so that it pinched in his waist. He started out the door. Halfway there he paused and thought better of it. He grabbed her toes, in an awkward gesture of intimacy. "Do you know what is happening to us?" he asked, and she thought he winced. He was out of the room like a shot, as if he were afraid to get an answer. She lay there and shivered, gripping the covers over her mouth, wondering why sexual bliss had left her so wretched and alert. She had presumed that pleasure of a certain order would give her back to herself. Instead she felt only a sense of loss, as if a limb had been cut off; and premonition, as if her future were at risk. She tried to put it down to the oddness of the event—a dark stripling appearing by moonlight, ushered in by wolves.

Marit got out of bed to find an extra comforter. If she was warm enough, she might conk out and sleep it off. As she raised the lid of the blanket chest, she remembered that he had not asked for another meeting. She let the lid fall, and began to make up her bed.

FOUR

C OLMAN M EYERLING, bishop of Hart County and
dean of Confessors and Martyrs in Ackroyd, Massachusetts,
was not a model for converts or new communicants. As a
shepherd of men, he was an uninviting figure. He scowled
down at the babies he baptized, as soon as smiled at them.
He stood watch by the beds of the dying with an eye on his
wristwatch. Bishop or not, he felt that his faith was his own
concern, and that religious matters ranked below ailments
and surgery as topics of conversation. He sneered at doe-
eyed devouts like his heir and nephew, Hugo, or glad-hand-
ers like his curate, Father Zack, who were walking human
billboards for the church.

The Bishop was a wiry small man with muscular arms

and legs. He had developed the muscles restraining big
hunters and polo ponies. In the First Great War he had
served as a cavalry officer. His mount had stumbled during
a charge at Herstal, and thrown him flat on his back on the
rocky Belgian field. When he was well again, his back had
healed into a hump, a hump like a hiker's pack, set up high
on his shoulders. People thought that he had joined the
clergy because of his fall, out of thanks to God for sparing
the life of a rake. They were not far wrong, but the hump,
not the fall, was the reason. He took his new appendage as a
sign of the sin in his nature, and held himself fortunate. The
run of men, looking into the mirror, see themselves whole
and unblemished, and are duped into thinking that their
souls are also intact. The Bishop's hump was the badge of
his continuing need for grace. Lest he forget that without
God's help he was less than a worm, he began to decorate
his hump, so that it should always be new to his attention
and his vain human eyes never tempted to smooth it out.
His clerical robes were layered with extra lace, sewn over
the hump. When he was at home, alone or receiving, he also
wore robes, loose caftans that came from Algeria, a country
he knew from his days as a sport and a hellion. These robes
were encrusted across the shoulders with panels of beading,
embroidered by a native tailor at his commission. His
parishioners assumed that he meant to disguise his hump; it
was the only vanity of his that they could pardon.

"That pagan temple up at Niles" they could not forgive. Wrestling Brewster, the Bishop's own deacon, had
been smuggling the cathedral account books home with him
for years, hoping and praying he could prove that Meyerling had been built with church funds. At last he found an

entry for a shipment of Vermont marble dating back to 1925, when Meyerling was rising from its foundations. When he discovered, by cross-checking the parish history, that repairs had been made that same year on the fonts and altars, Brewster began to gasp for air and fell off his desk chair in a faint. His attack was not a stroke, said the doctor, though it had all the earmarks.

Vlado and Luba Deym had played backgammon at Meyerling. They played for high stakes—Luba's sapphires; Vlado's Roman coins; or scraps from the Bishop's collection of antique laces. They played late into the summer nights, at a backgammon table set up on the marble terrace, which was lit by torches. A crimson awning, tilted up like a baldaquin, protected their heads from the heavy fall of dew. When the moon was bright, they looked down to a man-made lake and a gondola rocking gently by a little dock. The gondola had been painted gold, but the gilt was beginning to rub off. The Bishop had won the gondola in another backgammon tourney, played with the Countess Valmarana, on another marble terrace, overlooking the Brenta River.

Every summer, the Bishop hired the stroke from the Yale or Harvard crew to pole the golden barge around the pond wearing no covering above the waist but a red neckerchief. The strokes could not sing, so the Bishop applied to the Boston Conservatory, requesting poor Italian tenors who were studying there on scholarship. The gondola and half-naked gondolier irked local Yankee scruples more than the mansion itself, which was designed on a Palladian model, with the innovation of a colonnaded upper story. It pleased the Bishop to live outside his century, just as it saddened him that he had merely been born an Anglican. Since he could never wear a Cardinal's red hat, or be referred to as a Prince of the Church, he indulged his princely tastes at his summer cottage. To Vlado and Luba he was neither affected nor trivial. They were at home with him, since they had spent most of their youth at the courts of deposed crowned heads, in outposts more remote and provincial than Niles, Massachusetts.

During his last season at Niles, the Bishop received the summer colony on his deathbed; he held open house around the clock because he could not sleep. There was a cancer in his blood, which had drained the strength from his powerful trunk and limbs. Just his hands and his mind were active; he seemed to be all head and hands. He was living on grapes and cheese, and refused any medicine. Luba Deym often came to sit beside him in the early morning. She slept like a cat at night, dozing off for a matter of minutes and waking with a start, as if her name had been called. By 4 a.m., she was fretful and restless, so she would drive over to Meyerling, wearing her taffeta greatcoat with the Pierrot collar, and satin *pantoufles* with pointed toes that curled up backward. The pockets of her taffeta dressing gown were stuffed with treats and remedies like a grandmother's reticule. She carried a bar of the Bishop's favorite white chocolate, a bottle of hyssop water to refresh his forehead, and the pack of tarot cards that she was teaching him to read.

One morning she found him rapping his knuckles with the crucifix that he always held, a gesture which for a well man would have been like pacing the floor. There was a bitter smell in the room.

"Pouff, Colly, you have been burning paper. Surely it is dangerous."

"Hugo's letter," the Bishop rasped. "Hugo asks my permission to marry the Thielens girl."

"But he is a eunuch," said Luba firmly. She pronounced it "ainche," as if it were a French word.

"No, no," said the Bishop, "you are judging by his pasty complexion. They want to marry and have a tribe of pasty babies. They intend to turn Meyerling into a shelter for derelict men."

"You are not logical, Colly. She is Marian de Neufville's granddaughter."

"That does not alter their plans for my house!" the Bishop shouted.

Luba pulled the crucifix out of his grasp. She saw that his knuckles had started to bleed.

"Lie back, Colly." She took his hands. "Remember you are not helpless in this matter."

The Bishop's head sank deep into the goose-down pillows. His eyes were closed, but he was frowning like an angry vole. Luba massaged his hands and began to conspire out loud. As she spoke, the Bishop stopped frowning and opened his eyes. Then he asked to have his head propped up a little higher. Spite acted like iron in his blood. He took over the plot.

"So, now." He was summing up. "We will have blind children, not beggars. You and Vlado and the appalling Enos will be trustees. What a howling joke on a philanthropist. Hugo loses to charity."

Later that day the Bishop died, in much the same manner that he had lived. The World and the Faith stood flanking his bed, in the shape of a lawyer and a priest. In his right hand he held the crucifix, while Father Zachary read the office of extreme unction; with his left hand he initialed the clauses that changed his will.

On June 30th, unless it fell on a Sunday, the Meyerling Community held its Children's Fair. The fair marked the end of the spring term, and commemorated Bishop Meyerling's birthday. After the fair, the children were sent home to their families for two weeks. When they came back, Meyerling turned into a summer camp, which ran through Labor Day. The fair had opened at ten o'clock with a grand march. It was nearly noon.

Marit had been in the sanctuary all morning, walking the western edge of the enclosure, which bordered on Marco Jullian's pasturelands. Through the fence she could see his herd of fawn-colored Jerseys, which did not sense that a lynx could also watch them grazing. Marit had spotted the lynx stretched out on a low-hanging branch. He opened one eye, as if to measure the space between them. He could have felled her in one bound, but he rubbed his chin on the bark and went back to sleep. He preferred to nap by day and hunt at night, and, in any case, girls and cows were much too large—a red lynx likes to crunch on smaller prey. For an instant, when she had locked eyes with the lynx, Marit wondered if she was wise to go unarmed, but she hated guns and she felt that the animals knew who had one. A gun on her person would lend an extra vigilance, which would make the animals restless and defensive. Wearing a weapon implied that the beasts were not friends but enemies. She wanted to be their equal and their kinsman, and a gun was the badge of a jailer or a tyrant.

Jullian's pastures lay opposite—on a map of Marit's land—to the Meyerling blind school. It was here, on her side of the fence, that Marit had last caught sight of the two black bears, standing waist-deep in the pond and fishing for trout. Marit was tracking the bears by their spoor in order to find out what territory they had established. If there were no good hibernating spots in the black bears' territory, Herb Frechter, the local treeman, had promised to find some hollow tree trunks and deliver them to her. She had left a basket of currants by the edge of the pond, but the fruit was still uneaten. The bears had moved on. She could tell by the sun overhead that she had no time left today to go on searching.

With the sun climbing higher and higher, Marit dawdled back through the woods toward the sanctuary gate. She wanted to stay alone in her fenced-in wilderness, the only place in a peopled world where she was not afraid. The animals were equipped with killing claws and teeth; they could see at night and stalk her by her scent. They were larger or swifter than she was; a lynx could climb higher, and a bear could crush her with its weight. But four-footed creatures wanted nothing from her, except that she should not harm them. Her two-legged kind had hidden needs, which they expected her to understand.

Marit's senses shut down outside this fence, and her reflexes played her false. Her instinct about any animal was sure and generous. She could tell the growl of pleasure from the growl of warning. She knew when a bite was playful, or a signal that her hands had touched a sore place under the fur. Several times she had felt the power that belongs to healers, and had seen a black ring or aura encircling the bodies of creatures who had shown no prior signs of illness. Her special sight had helped to halt the infection before it grew.

What power she had to help her animals came from love untrammeled by suspicion, the kind of love that does not seek its own advantage, or negotiate for favorable terms. With human beings her insight foundered in mistrust. When animals bared their fangs, they were enraged; in humans a show of teeth was called a smile. A freak of weather could make an animal erratic, or a tumor pressing in upon the brain; but human actions were always uncertain and perplexing, especially the actions of the people whom she wished to love. Marit had come to expect injustice and whim in all relations, and only Lola had ever loved her without reserve. She had learned early to be on guard against her mother, before she was old enough to go to school.

A baby brother, who was not named, had died at birth. Luba stayed in her room and did not call for Marit. She may have asked for Vlado, but Vlado had disappeared. Marit sat on the stairs where she could watch Luba's bedroom door, and the train of maids and nurses moving in and out, bearing trays of food and other trays covered with cloths. The nurses never closed the door without shaking their heads, or lifting a finger to their lips to keep Marit from speaking. Sometimes they sent her away and she would visit the nursery, which had been painted light blue and refurnished for a new baby boy.

After several weeks Luba had come down to take her meals, but Marit was kept in the playroom until her mother had retired. Twice she tried to sneak into the dining room, but her governess caught her in time and dragged her upstairs. Marit had seen the shadows under Luba's eyes and her pale, thin mouth, and she knew, without being told, that her mother was mourning.

Marit knew what dying meant, because her own star-nosed mole had just died, the mole who lived in a shoe box under her bed. Now the mole could not eat or move or play with a string. Its eyes were closed and its coat was matted and dull. Marit wished to share her sadness with her mother, but she was not allowed to talk to her or go near her. The best she could do, for their mutual comfort, was to put the mole in one of her socks with its head sticking out, and carry it into the nursery. She lay the creature in her brother's cradle and pulled the embroidered sheet up to its head. She never heard Luba enter, nor could she remember whether Luba had hit her first and thrown the mole out of the window afterward, or the other way around. She did remember lying on the nursery rug until it was dark, with one hand cupping her swollen cheek, and her knees drawn under her chin. Her tears washed the blood off the corners of her mouth, ran down her neck, and stained her white collar brown. When her governess saw the collar, she was very angry.

Marit stood at the edge of the woods where the land had been cleared. She could see the gate in the distance across the field. The sun was hot and the ground was stubbly with new growth. She stopped to tie her shoes and roll up her sleeves. On her way to the gate she stopped for one thing and another: to uproot a sapling that had grown too high;

to pick some chicory that would not reach the house alive; to build a pile of rocks next to a patch of poison ivy, so that she could find it when she came back later to burn it out. The Children's Fair had started by now; still she dragged her feet. Gabriel would be at the fair, and she did not know how he would treat her.

Gabriel had come to her house twice in the last six days, with the lapse of a day between each visit. The first time he came around nine at night, without calling beforehand. He did not use the bell or the door knocker, either; he tapped on a windowpane. He asked if she had found his Swiss Army knife, and stayed quite briefly. One of his pupils had frequent nightmares, and he did not like to be out too long. He inquired about her wolves politely, as if they were parents or relatives. There was some conversation about raising animals, and whether it was easier or harder than teaching children, but Marit was so bewildered that her answers were curt. He had discovered that she was a Meyerling trustee, and asked her if the board would consider endowing a fund for blind black children. While he held forth on the democracy of blindness, she watched his strong, square hands and well-shaped forearms. His dark hair had auburn lights and his nose was curved like a hawk's. When he left, after a cordial handshake, she was numb with shame. He was a grown-up man, with a storehouse of ideals and goals, while she had showed herself for a rampant, lustful primitive, sitting mute, with parted lips, eyeing the shape of his penis in his trousers, transmitting greedy thought-waves which had offended him and driven him away.

The second time he did not call, ring, knock, or tap. He

threw a shower of gravel at the window, a noise which startled her, then roused her anger. When she opened the door, she did not take stock of his perfect teeth or his cleft chin; she noticed that he was shorter than she was by at least three inches. She blocked the doorway, waiting for him to speak, but she had not counted on this new, commanding Gabriel, who took hold of her and kissed her deeply, bending her backward to correct the difference in their heights, holding her with one arm and closing the door with the other hand. As he guided her across the floor toward the velvet sofa, his mouth never left her mouth, except to murmur that he should not be there, that he thought he loved her. Marit yielded to his heat and haste and closed her eyes. For once she had nothing to do; he did all the work. He had the silken touch of a craftsman; in his hands zippers slid open, elastic did not snap, and buttons melted out of their holes. Marit was opening and melting, too; there was a buzzing sound in her head, the sound the television makes when a station goes off the air. Once in a while her mind formed a thought, in spite of itself, like the awareness that her navel was as sensitive as her breasts. She felt her shirt slipping off her shoulders, and waited for Gabriel to take her arms out of the sleeves.

Instead the scene began playing backward, as if some-one had flipped the reverse switch on a projector: her shirt was pulled up, and her trousers, which had been piled on the floor around her feet, were drawn back over her legs and belted at the waist. Her heart fluttered in alarm. What had she done to make him change his mind? Her underwear was plain and mended, but she kept herself clean. Or per-haps she had been too passive; she had heard that some men want a woman to move like a mink. Gabriel's hands were still working, smoothing, buttoning, and tucking, making her shipshape before he lifted her to her feet. She did not open her eyes until his arms released her, in time to see him turn and run out the front door.

Marit made her way up the meadow toward the house, walking as if she were wearing lead shoes. Any moment Lola would arrive to take her to the fair, and start to scold her for being late and dirty. Her mind was simmering like a witch's kettle, full of eyeless dreads. She did not want to deal with Gabriel in the light of day; she did not even know which Gabriel would confront her, the skittish one or the suave one. He had been tossing her in a blanket, and she was not sure if she had landed on her feet or on her head. She was too proud to hover around him, and too muddled to ask herself why she should be frightened of a man whom she had known for less than a week. She felt like a convalescent, and the sight of him might hasten her cure or bring on a relapse. When she got to the fair, she would stake him out and keep her distance.

She could not keep her distance from the blind children, however, as much as she might want to. They knew their way through the terraces and the lemon arbors. They strayed in groups on the reachless lawns below, like the sheep that the Bishop had kept to mow the grass. Marit thought of deer when she thought of the Meyerling children, the fallow deer in the Dangerfield Zoo. The herd of five had been beaten with chains by an unknown vandal. Marit had driven to the zoo the day the newspaper story had appeared. Only two deer were left. Three were critically wounded in the sick bay. They were like fairy deer, quite defenseless in their pen, which had low sides and gave them no protection from their attacker. Perhaps their small size and helplessness had provoked his cruelty. They had fleet legs and light frames for outrunning predators, but they had nowhere to run in that tight, low pen. She had sat for hours on a bench across from their pen: their frailty made her feel tentative; they would have to be handled gently, for fear of bruising them. A person unbalanced or mad, watching them as she did, might experience that tentativeness as an itch crawling on his skin. His confusion might become frustration and turn into rage.

The fallow deer were like the blind. But the pity the blind inspired in Marit made her hesitant and clumsy, so that she mistimed her instructions when she was guiding them. She would tell them to step up on the curb just too soon or too late. They would miss their footing, and turn on her when they stumbled.

Marit pitied blind people, but she was also frightened of them. The deaf became fierce; they resisted their handicap. The blind had no choice but to surrender to their condition; they had to learn to live by a new set of rules entirely. Their submissiveness lent them an aspect of humility that she did not trust. The blind were set apart, like saints, but their saintliness was an accident, not a choice. Marit suspected that the blind had invented a secret code and language, that they met by themselves and laid plans for the undoing of the sighted world. She did not know where their meeting places might be, but she felt that if there were such places they should be found and rooted out with the same purpose that inspires those horticultural zealots who pour kerosene down into mole holes. If the blind were to gather in large numbers, their hidden rage would become their collective resource. Because they could not see, they had an edge on clairvoyance and telepathy. They would gather, focus their rage, and beam out its killing rays.

It seemed to Marit that the blind had no spiritual guidance. They were only taught how to measure out space, how to learn the measurements of the material world so that they could "pass" for sighted. The very process of their rehabilitation taught them to dissemble. Their loss of sight could develop into extra-sightedness, but they were never told that this talent could be used for good or for evil.

Marit had stopped in her tracks. Her head hung down and her arms hung at her sides. She was flicking her thumbnail inside the nail of her ring finger, making a regular sound like the timer on a homemade bomb. A voice up above, at the house, made her lift her head. Lola was striding down the hill to get her. She was as cross as two sticks.

"You do this every year. You think you're so brave, making yourself go, but I have to drag you. You should resign; they have plenty of trustees."

She advanced on Marit, who was standing fixed to the path. There were leaves in her hair. Lola fluffed up her hair and began to pick them out.

"What's this sticky mess on your cheek? You look as if you've been eating your grandmother."

"I have awful thoughts," said Marit. "I hate my thoughts."

"If you cry, you'll just get red eyes and look more like an animal. Now hustle on up to the house and get cleaned off."

Marit stood in front of her closet, riffling through the clothes hangers. She took out a pair of white flannel slacks that had belonged to Vlado. She had had his trousers cut down to her size, and all his silk shirts and blazers. The shirts had red coronets worked into the cuffs.

"Are you trying to rile me?" asked Lola. She grabbed the white flannels away from Marit and threw them on the bed. "You can look like a girl this once. Get out the black floral."

"I will not wear stockings," said Marit. "I will not be bound around the waist."

"You are a lady, and a trustee, and you're going to act like one."

It was easier to give in to Lola than to make a fuss. Lola pulled off her clothes in swift strokes, like a nurse removing bandages. She dropped the full-skirted dress over Marit's head and stuffed her arms into the sleeves. She pushed a garter belt and stockings into her hands, and walked her to the bathroom.

"Wash your face, now, and fix your hair. Bend over to brush it the way I showed you. I want you to look all fresh and flouncy for your new beau."

Marit made Lola drive Luba's old Continental to Meyerling. She sat as stiff as a doll in the passenger seat and looked straight ahead.

"Are you cross with me, darlin'?" asked Lola. "Or do you have a stiff neck?"

"I feel as if I'm made of glass. When I get dressed up, if a breeze blows a hair out of place, the whole image is broken."

"God made me a lady and you a tomboy," Lola sighed. "I think he got us scrambled."

"You stick by me at the fair," said Marit. "I don't want you to leave my side."

"I'd like to be helpful, honey. Can't you bear in mind that they're only piss-and-vinegar kids?"

"They make me feel doomed," said Marit.

Lola shook her head. She turned right at the Meyerling gate and followed the arrows that pointed toward the car park.

It was a blue day, without clouds, and the light had a seaside glare. The crowd was large, and the women wore straw hats and white gloves, as if they had been invited to a garden party. Folding tables lined the wide gravel paths of the Bishop's lemon garden, displaying the upper school's art show, the middle school's raised geological map of the Berkshire Mountains, and the clay ashtrays, lumpy pot holders, and pewter bowls made by the craft classes.

Around the basin of the fountain at the center of the garden were a group of cages pinned with red and blue ribbons. Inside the cages crouched New Zealand white and red satin rabbits, which had won the ribbons at the last Hart County Fair. Marit forgot her nerves and kneeled down to look at the rabbits. A little boy came up beside her and offered her a scrap of lettuce. It dismayed and touched her that he had known where she was kneeling, that he had held out the lettuce at the level of her hand. He looked like an ordinary boy, rather fat and pug-nosed, the kind of boy whose shirttails are always straggling out of his pants.

She pushed the leaf through the wire and twitched it at the rabbit. The rabbit jumped to the back of the cage and sat there shivering.

"They scare easy," said the little boy. "Raccoons would be a lot more fun."

Marit was startled by his response, but it made her smile.

"Why do you keep them?" she asked.

"Mr. Dufton says they're safe for blind children because they're gentle."

"They're supposed to be gentle," said Marit, "but you have scratches all over your arms."

"Oh, don't tell him, please promise," said the boy. "I told him I was scratched by blackberries. I'd rather have rabbits than nothing."

Marit took his fat hand in both of hers.

"I promise," she said. "All animals scratch sometimes. It's because they can't tell us what they want."

Until she saw the rabbit cages, Marit had kept a claw-like grip on Lola's arm. Now she turned around and looked up and down the walks, but Lola was not at any of the display tables. There was always a feeding trough at the fair, so it would not be a chore to find her. Down on the lawn was a yellow tent with the children's bakery banner drooping between two poles in front of it. The bakery was Mr. Dufton's most publicized scheme; it had made his reputation as a therapist and a pedagogue. "These little folks must learn the useful arts," he had confided to journalists; "they will be leaving our haven for the bitter world of work." There was no chance that these children of the rich would ever work for their living, but no one, reporters or trustees, had questioned his vocational program. During a lull in one board meeting, Marit had suggested that he expand the program to include auto mechanics and television repair. She had been reproached at length for her sarcasm, and quite rightly. The bakery was a success, and even made a profit. The children had learned to run it by themselves; every student, big or little, worked a daily shift. They made two kinds of cookies, peanut applesaucers and chocolate snickerdoodles, and a kind of hard oaten health bread that had to be cut with a carving knife. County grocery stores sent in a weekly order, and souvenir shops displayed the baked goods alongside pine-needle pillows and autumn leaves laminated in plastic.

Marit left the chubby keeper standing guard over his prize rabbits, and walked down to the tent across the grass, instead of by the pathway. She poked her head into the tent, looked around, and caught Lola doing an amazing thing. Four adolescents manned the long table, a plank set on sawhorses. Besides the giant nut-studded cookies, they were selling ice cream and lemonade. Lola had bought a cup of vanilla, which she held in one hand. With her free hand, she was spooning out the ice cream and spreading it over the surface of a saucer-sized cookie which was clamped in her jaws. She could hardly greet Marit in that state, so she waved her spoon.

"I ask and beg of you," said Marit, laughing. "Here, give me the cup."

Lola bit off one section of iced cookie and munched it down.

"It's a good place for hogging," she whispered. "None of them can see me."

They left the tent and continued down the lawn, heading for the tennis courts at the bottom of the slope. The tennis courts were likely to be deserted; only the teachers used them, and they were busy supervising the fair. Lola wanted to smoke a cigarette off by herself. She had a code about smoking. Indoors was acceptable, except between courses at a dinner party. Outdoors, in a public place, was incorrect. There was a special clause in the code for New York City: one never lit up on the flossy sections of Park Avenue.

"You're the girl nobody knows," said Marit, who loved to devil her. "You're nine-tenths underwater, like an iceberg. Who could guess that you like to kiss girls and eat like a pig? Would you like to keep our friendship a secret, too? Would that give you a charge?"

"Be sweet," said Lola, squeezing Marit's waist. "It's too nice a day to be told I'm a yellow coward."

"Pick up the pace," said Marit, "and don't look right or left. I've got Horty to starboard and I'm not sure whether she's seen us."

"Where is she?" asked Lola.

"More or less up by the tent."

"We might lose her," said Lola, "except that I'm a magnet to Horty. She thinks I know all about Life."

"Oh, ho," Marit teased her. "Is Horty an armchair sapphic?"

Horty Waite was a matron of their age, who wanted to know them. Horty had the soul of a tag-along. She must have been the original wait-for-me child. Besides a growing number of streaky-blond sons and daughters, she bred bassets—brindle bassets—which were registered on the rolls of the Northeastern Kennel Club. Horty was floppy and mournful herself, from being left out of things. Poor Horty was usually pregnant, but even when she wasn't, she wore two damp spots on her shirtfronts. This state of perpetual lactation was not attractive. It was Lola's theory that she also nursed the bassets.

Horty was a nice enough egg, not so much dim as simple. In any case, her brain had been wired wrong; there were odd short circuits and misfirings in the system. It was just as well that she never listened to what she was saying. If she had, Lola and Marit would have been deprived of a favorite pleasure. They had begun to keep lists of the curious dysphasic things that Horty said, but dysphasia is a pathological condition, and Horty's scrambling of commonplace images was more of a gift, like being able to make a piece of chalk write on a blackboard by itself. "That whelp was covered with eczema from toe to foot." "Muffet turned on me and I had to fight her off hoof, nail, and claw." "I raised that bitch from a puppy; I can't just give her the hatchet!" It wasn't malice that inspired their collecting; it was pure delight. But every nugget of gold cost them two or three hours of dog talk, and today they did not feel like paying so steep a price.

The lawn sloped down to a miniature bluff overlooking the courts. This steep bank was planted with yew trees, pruned flat across the tops, and grown so thickly together that their branches formed a kind of screen. Marit led the way around the yew screen and turned sideways to make the descent. All at once she dropped to the ground like a soldier under fire. On her elbows she crawled back behind the yews and hissed at Lola. She sat down and put her head between her knees, in the position that is believed to stave off a faint. Lola was stunned. She began to move toward the edge of the yews.

"Get in here. They can see you," Marit hissed.

Lola looked down at the courts. A man was sitting on one of the benches, facing away from them. He had his arm around a girl, or woman, whose head was bowed.

"I admire your discretion," said Lola, "but I fail to see why you're acting like an afflicted ape."

Marit was sitting with her arms over her ears, rocking and whimpering.

"I feel sick," she kept saying, "I feel sick. I'm going to be sick."

With her arms still wrapped around her head, she looked up at Lola. Her face was pinched and monkey-like, too, and her eyes were enormous.

"Is he kissing her?" she begged. "Are they kissing? Look and see if they're kissing!"

Like a true friend, Lola entered into Marit's mood. She forced a section of yew apart and made herself a peephole.

"For what it's worth," said Lola, peering through it, "he's patting her head."

"What else?" pleaded Marit. "Don't stop watching. I have to know!"

"No," said Lola. She let the branches snap back and crouched down next to Marit. She shook her by the chin. Tears were streaming out of Marit's eyes, which were screwed tight shut.

"Open your eyes," ordered Lola, "and look at me. I want you to stop this. You're having some kind of a fit. Anyone but me would think you were crazy."

"I feel killed," whispered Marit. "I could kill him."

Lola pulled Marit into her arms and held her close.

"Oh, honey, I am so sorry. I'm not very swift. You had me so rattled that I never made the connection."

All the breath went out of Marit. She nearly toppled Lola, who had to adjust her footing to support her.

"I'm a dupe. I'm a dupe and a patsy. I want to die."

"That's enough, now." Lola made her sit up. She put

her hands under Marit's armpits and yanked her to her feet. With one arm around her, she made her walk a few steps in one direction. Then she turned her around and made her walk the opposite way. When Marit seemed to be standing on her own, she led her up to the yew screen. She opened the peephole again, and made Marit hold back the branches on her side.

"You do the looking," she said. Marit hung her head. "Be your own voyeur; I dare you. Now tell me exactly what you see."

Marit opened and closed her mouth, but no sound came out.

"Stop impersonating a retard," snapped Lola. "Tell me what they're doing."

"Lola," said Marit in a whisper, "she's really young. She has her hair in pigtails. Lola? There's a book on her lap. She has her hands on the pages."

"Braille," confirmed Lola. "Where is he?"

"He . . ." Marit's voice began to falter.

"Say 'Gabriel,' " Lola directed, "if that's who he is."

"Gabriel"—Marit paused, for the space of two beats, or three—"is on the bench. At the other end, with his arms folded. He is tapping his foot."

"That's exciting," said Lola. "I'm just sweating from excitement. Have they got their clothes on?"

"You lay off me," said Marit, and aimed an elbow at Lola's ribs. She pressed her lips together, trying not to smile, but the smile got the better of her. Her face was a regular mess. She had blackened her eyelashes and the Mascara was running down her cheeks and collecting in raccoon patches under her eyes.

"I have to sit down again," she said. "I'm all right, but I feel like I've been caught in a rockslide."

"You also look it," said Lola, stepping up to the peep-hole. "I'll take over here. I might take up spying as a hobby."

Marit lay back on the grass, with one hand on her chest and the other on her abdomen. She filled her lungs with air and let the breath out very slowly, until she could feel her belly caving in. She thought that ten deep, rolling breaths would make her calmer. Deep breathing had worked for Vlado in 1949, when he learned that the People's Republic of Hungary had annexed the Deym lands and turned the castle into a reconditioning center for political prisoners. In order to sleep at night, Vlado had hired a Yoga master. The sessions were held behind the double sliding doors on the living-room floor. Marit, at age fifteen, had been eager to learn. She might have become more proficient in the discipline if Yogi Nebelsine's elastic trunks had not been so brief or his head so domed, or the hair on his back so pubic and abundant.

"Ho ho," said Lola, startling Marit in mid-exhalation. "She may be young, but she's choice. Full of tactile values. All that downy peach bloom; the French have a better word —duvet. My, I do love a swelling calf and a tapering ankle."

Lola had craned her neck partway through the branches. Marit had an urge to get up and push her all the way through.

"Can't you leave me be? Do you want to get me more stirred up?"

"Don't you fret. Old Gabriel is completely immune to the peach bloom. They're doing remedial reading. She seems to be a little slow."

"He's not touching her anymore, is he?"

"Well, she keeps covering her face with her hands, and then he slaps her hands back on the page. I'd teach her not to be so stubborn with me."

Marit began to beat the ground with her hands and feet. "You're trying to hurt me. If you want her, he must want her too!"

"You watch your temper. At least you'll never see me making myself sick with jealousy over one puny human."

Marit sat up straight. It seemed to her that she was hearing something important.

"Jealous? Is that what I am?"

Lola looked back at her sharply. Marit sat there, frowning and slack-jawed. Under the force of revelation, she seemed more slow-witted than enlightened.

"I'd like to know what else," said Lola. "You came unhinged."

"I've been jealous," Marit started to argue. "I was jealous of Marcy Gammons at school, when she got editor of the magazine. But I didn't feel as if my ribs had been crushed."

"You have the emotional vocabulary of a five-year-old. That was envy."

"Marit." Lola wiped her hands, which were tacky with pitch. "I love you and you can damn well listen to me." She stood in front of Marit and towered over her; she would not condescend to hunker down and plead.

"You had me good and frightened. You know how it is when you are very sick? You belong to the germ. Jealousy took you right over, honey; it ate you up. Your pretty face changed; your body changed too. You looked like someone with terminal arthritis, all pinched and bent."

"I don't work right. I'm ugly inside. Is that what you mean?"

Marit cried black tears down her cheeks. Lola kneeled down beside her.

"I wish I had a mirror. I'd give you a shock that would last you the rest of your life."

They heard voices, one low-pitched and one high, from behind the yews. Both girls froze in place until the voices veered away. Gabriel and his student were walking up the slope. Marit could see his falcon's profile, and the tendrils of hair at the back of his neck, which were feathery from sweat and from the breeze that had started to blow. She could make out the line of his hips and his large workman's hands. Watching him before, through the gap in the yew trees, his perfections had hurt her, like thorns rammed into her forehead and spears jabbed into her heart. She had no spunk left now for hurting or for admiring. The man who was walking up the hill was very short. The short man climbing the slope looked like a boy.

It was time to go home and change back into trousers. She had traps to repair, the kind of trap that encloses and does not wound the animal. When the traps were fixed, she was going to bait them with nuts. There were cases of rabies in the county and squirrels were carriers. Marit would take some trapped squirrels to the zoo, where they could be tested.

She reached out her hands and Lola pulled her to her feet. They did not have to go back to the car by way of the fair. There was a path through the woods behind the tennis courts that led to the field which was being used as a parking lot. Marit held herself unsteadily at first, like a vase with a hairline crack in it. She leaned on Lola's arm until they had crossed the courts.

When they found the car, Marit got into the driver's seat. She liked to drive with bare feet, so she handed her shoes to Lola. She drove over the bumpy field and waved to the guard at the entrance as she turned down the road. She felt well enough now to engage in a little mischief. When her nerve was intact, she drove like a teenage boy, left elbow clamped down on the door and fingers playing lightly on the steering wheel. Her right arm was stretched out on the seat back. She pinched Lola's shoulder.

"Don't tweak me," said Lola, "hold the wheel. You're driving by remote control."

"I can drive with my knee," answered Marit. "You want me to show you?"

Lola made an Italian gesture and collapsed against the seat.

"Why can't you be a moderate person? Why can't you be placid? You're always on the edge of this or the verge of that. Oh, the peace of a partial lobotomy! One tiny nick in the frontal lobe. Think how quiet and useful you could be."

Marit had no choice but to steer with both hands, she was laughing so hard. Up ahead was the East Niles common, and a yellow blinker.

Marit slowed down and looked over at Lola, whose eyes were closed.

"You've never had an attack," she said, "like me, today."

Lola roused herself.

"I've been angry enough to hit out, but I've never gone under. Anger kills my feelings. If my girl wants somebody else, there must be something wrong with her. Nothing wrong with me, that's for sure. I'm the best there is."

Between East Niles and Niles there was heavy late-afternoon traffic, people coming home from work and chartered buses bringing vacationers from the city. Marit was restless in traffic, and apt to grow unruly, passing cars in no-passing zones and tailgating white-haired drivers. Lola watched her to see if she was about to break any rules. For once, she seemed to be content with the enforced slow pace. She was frowning, but the frown was thoughtful, not impatient.

"Luba said that men have more glands than women." Marit spoke without taking her eyes away from the road. "She told me that women want men to admire them, but men need to have a woman for their health. If they stay with one woman, they get thin and lose their hair. Like Vlado, I suppose she meant."

"What does that make me?" asked Lola. "I like to stick to one girl at a time."

"She said that expecting a man to be faithful was like expecting a pig to smell sweet. They want a woman without seeing her face, if she has on a tight skirt or high heels. She said the first thing they do is undress you in their minds."

"Will you kindly stop saying 'she said'? I thought you told me that Luba liked to make up stories to scare you."

"Just horror stories at bedtime, but she knew about men. She had a lover."

"You kept that one a secret. Who was he?"

"The French consul or the Swedish chargé. I imagine both."

Lola wished that Marit would look at her instead of

staring ahead. She did not want this conversation to get too earnest.

"I'd say that Luba had the extra glands, and she fed you that old-country moonshine to keep you off her tail. Better to have you blame the whole male sex than your poor wronged mother."

They were out of Niles and on the open road. The faster she drove, the livelier Marit looked. She turned to Lola with an impish expression on her face.

"Do you think that Gabriel has extra glands?"

"I hope so. You sure won't have any fun if he has too few."

The approach to the Deym estate was banked with mock orange. Marit breathed in their scent, which was sweeter on still, warm days. She turned in to the circular driveway and stopped the motor.

"I guess I'm staying for supper," said Lola. "It's not shredded wheat again, is it?"

"Mrs. Mayo was here this afternoon. She said that she'd leave shepherd's pie."

"I love a nursery supper. Can we make some pink junket, too?"

"Stay off food just a second," begged Marit. "I need you to listen to me. I want Gabriel. I want it to be perfect. What if it doesn't work?"

Lola patted her cheek and started to open the door. "Love is an appetizer, honey; it's not supposed to be the whole meal. It's the zest to life, you catch? It's not life itself."

Marit gave up. She pushed down the door handle on her side. If she wanted Lola's attention, she would have to feed her.

FIVE

A NATIVE of Niles, Massachusetts, would describe himself as living "in town," and any summer resident as living "on the hill." There was no town unless you counted the general store, the post office, and Rippey's Yard Goods, and the two and a half new bungalows in the field behind them, set down by a builder who ran out of funds before the third house was finished. There was no hill, either, at least not in the feudal sense, no high ground occupied by the overlord who could see his enemies coming better from a height. The whole landscape around Niles was hilly, and the hills rose up and dipped down without regard for the wealth or ancestry of any householder. The terrain was democratic, if the natives were not.

Vladimir and Luba Deym had lived "on the hill" for

twenty-five years. They were considered hill dwellers even during the last years before their deaths, when they had closed up the New York apartment, canceled their standing Easter reservation at the Paris Ritz, and moved to Niles for the sake of Vlado's lungs. The Berkshires are damp and rainy, but he breathed better there than he did in the bad city air.

The distance between the townspeople and the summer colony was congenial to Vlado. He did not like much society of any kind. He preferred to stay in the attic with his inventions, the automatic cigarette smoker, the dog-tick plucker, and the can of shaving cream that produced hot lather years before its time. It was not clear whether or not Vlado wanted his inventions to work. He had drawn plans for the shaving-cream can down to the last detail, recorded the results of many successful tests, and then stuffed the records and the spidery drawings into a dress box. He spent years, by contrast, building the cigarette smoker, which stood by itself in one of the attic cells. It looked like a whimsical piece of motorized sculpture, and ran intermittently, but never for more than an hour. Vlado's most successful invention, the Bishop liked to remark, was prolonging his time alone in the attic.

It made Luba petulant to be consigned to the hill by the townspeople. She complained of it, remembering Hungary: "We had so kind a relation with our peasants." Luba watched the summer colonists at the post office making up to the postmistress, Anna Weebs, asking her advice about carpenters or yard boys, getting her to top the weather report with an even gloomier prediction. These conversations seemed stagy and impersonal to Luba, who preferred to gossip. With the natural impertinence of the aristocrat, she questioned Mrs. Weebs about her daughter's acne, and lectured her on the abuse of sugar in the American diet. When next she went to Manhattan, she brought back a bottle of astringent solution from her Hungarian faceman, and presented it to Mrs. Weebs for young Roseanne. "We Hungarians have an ancient knowledge of the complexion," Luba explained; "send her to me, I will release the pores." Anna Weebs was used to the aloof cajolery of the hill dwellers; she had no defense against Luba's imperious brand of friendliness. Rosie Weebs spent many hours on the chaise longue in Luba's bedroom, waiting for a green paste of herbs to do its work. The spots on her face dimmed down from red to pink, and Luba gave her a pair of white cotton gloves to wear to bed, so that she would not pick her face while she was sleeping.

Luba embraced village life that one and only summer. The embrace was strenuous, and smothered any resistance. She spread her arms wide and took East Niles, as well as Niles, to her bosom. Only the faintest demurrals could be heard, but not by Luba. No sound came out of Mr. Hinning's mouth when he opened the side door of his Unitarian church, ready to lock up for the day, and found Luba and a crew of nurserymen on their hands and knees, pressing down bark chips around a dozen rosebushes they had planted in a double semicircle facing the door. Fratelli's truck was parked in front of the church, and Mr. Hinning saw two men unloading a wrought-iron bench that had been painted white. At this point he began to agitate his hand in the air. Luba saw the gesture and read it as a salute. "There you are, Vicar, you will be so pleased! We are putting a meditation garden." Mr. Hinning backed up the steps and stumbled inside the church building. It is likely that he slammed the door behind him.

After this, Luba's village summer moved into high gear. Besides a gift of the German classics, untranslated, to the one-room library, her legacy to Niles was the redecoration of the old Grange Hall, in disuse since local farmers were now in the resort business. The Grange would become the center for town sociables, and Luba herself, with her dimpled knuckles, would wield the gavel at Tuesday Great Books, at the Seeders and Weeders on Thursday afternoons, and at the Birdwalkers, which met on no schedule, but often and quarrelsomely.

Out went the backless wooden benches, and in their place were installed a vanload of Windsor chairs, tied up with quilted cushions in a green-and-white bamboo print. "Can't we stop it? She'll quilt the walls!" muttered Mrs. Rippey, whose yard-goods store had not been patronized. The walls were safe, but the century-old rafters were not. Luba wanted to paint them green, with white mottoes on them, to carry out the color scheme of the cushions. Now the local muttering turned into mutiny. A squadron of clubwomen, led by Sarah Rippey, barred the doors to the painters, who made a hasty retreat with their tarps and ladders.

Luba's revenge on the purists was transcendent. Ferreting through the area, she grabbed up a motley huge battery of Colonial kitchen equipment—keelers and cheese presses, pestles without mortars, slices and churns, posnets, skellets and toasting forks—and hung them all, out of reach, on Early American nails. Having turned the Grange into a nightmare historical society, she took an early-morning train to Saratoga Springs, where mineral baths and deep massage drained the mischief out of her.

By the afternoon of the first Animal Airlift fund-raising cof-fee, the bamboo print had faded to a nameless zigzag, and the Americana had been donated, on Marit's orders, to the Dangerfield museum. Thirty or forty people sat in the Windsor chairs, which had been drawn up close to the stage in uneven rows, listening to the speaker, whose voice carried so well that most of the audience edged its chairs backward when he started to talk.

". . . to preserve wild animals that have strayed into the asphalt jungles of Pittsfield and Albany, forced to subsist on rotting garbage, murdered by delinquents and speeding cars. . . ."

George Schulte, helicopter pilot, stretched out his arms with an evangelical flourish, long arms that spanned a row of boxes behind which he stood as he delivered the opening pitch.

". . . raccoons, opossums, foxes, squirrels, owls, hawks, and nonpoisonous snakes," he continued, slapping the top of each box in turn, causing a scrambling or a yawping inside, except where the blue racer lay coiled.

". . . humanely trapped and flown by my team to the woody recesses of the Tri-State National Forest and the Deym Sanctuary . . ."

Marit stood in the back of the hall, next to the curtain hung for voters in town-council elections. Stewart Odell, who taught chemistry at the high school, was pulling at the sleeve of her jacket and talking in an audible whisper. He was urging that the Airlift be given an acronym, which could not be AA, and just as certainly not BAA (Berkshire Animal Airlift). Stewart pressed up too close to people when he spoke to them. Marit could see the thinning hair behind his ears, and the red marks left by his glasses; it made her want to pound lumps on him.

"You spray when you talk," said Marit, backing away. "Perhaps your bite needs adjusting. You must ask your dentist."

George Schulte produced a toy model of a helicopter, convinced that the rustics in the audience had never seen one, and waved it over the boxes, whirling the propeller with one finger to illustrate his points. George talked like a press release, or a brochure. Marit tried to remember who had suggested that he be the principal speaker.

Several whispering duos had formed by the partial shelter of the homemade election booth. Eleanor Stoeber was head-to-head with Sarah Rippey. Apparently, Eleanor had missed an episode of *A Silver Lining*.

". . . it showed up on the brain scan. Dr. Mac wants to do more tests before he tells Andrea."

"No," breathed Eleanor. "She has a concert tour ahead of her!"

Marit caught Lola's voice, and then she heard Horty Waite's. She leaned in to pick up the thread.

". . . the only girl I've ever met who made a profit on her abortion."

"How could she?" asked Horty.

"Very simple," said Lola severely. "She collected five hundred dollars from all four of them."

In the front row across the aisle sat Moira Raymer, who wrote the social notes for the Dangerfield *Beacon*. Marit recognized her felt beret and the shell-studded glasses on a chain around her neck. A pad lay open on her lap, but she was not writing notes on the Airlift. She was counting the money in her wallet, spreading the bills out in fan formation, like a hand of cards.

Marit had asked the *Beacon* to send their nature writer —anyone but Moira, who was campaigning in print to get the Deym preserve opened to the public, on the model of Mott's Jungle Joyride in Oneco, New Hampshire. Marit had paid one visit to Mott's, where the tourists were driven around in zebra-striped vans and warned, if they valued their lives, not to roll down the windows. Most of them paid no attention, so the driver was forced to brake for a party of apes, who were fighting in the middle of the road over a bag of popcorn. These same apes later climbed on the van, waving empty bottles, and beat a tattoo on the roof while the women and children shrieked. The apes were thin, the lion was shedding, and the hyena was covered with scales. Marit had wanted to feed the Motts and Moira to those wretched animals; red meat would soon correct the symptoms of malnutrition.

Marit moved a few steps forward. She was trying to calculate the attention span of the rest of the seated audience. It was not much greater. Every person she saw was knitting, shifting, groping in a handbag, or working on his cuticles. The Airlift committee members, sitting in the second row, were passing wrapped candies back and forth. George Schulte was writing the Airlift budget on an easel blackboard.

Then she felt the itch. The spackle of red pinpricks on the insides of her wrists was not caused by her rough linen sleeves. Marit was literally allergic to fools. The Animal Airlift had been her idea; it was out of her hands now. She was democrat enough to know that work gets done when the workers make it their own, but the autocrat in her chafed at the wrists. The Airlift had turned into a living village satire, and she was playing a stock-in-trade character, the Patroness.

These dozers, knitters, and cuticle pickers thought that the suffering of wild animals extended to worms and flea-bite, and that their peril could be annulled by placing "Deer Crossing" signs on two-way roads. She remembered Dr. De-vane, the gentleman vet, refusing to splint the leg of a hurt raccoon that she had brought him in a cat-carrier. Marit had spent hours watching that coon, sauntering on his unbroken hind legs, longer than his front legs, elevated in back like the rigged chassis of a stock car.

"Better put him down, Marit, you're a good shot."

"I'm paying for it, god damn it! Pretend he's a cocker spaniel!"

"Let him go, Marit. Wild things cure themselves some-times."

She had splinted the raccoon's leg herself, in an agony for both of them, the splint fastened on knock-kneed, and Marit's fingers bitten to the bone from forcing painkillers down his throat. He had limped away and she had searched the property for days, finding him dead, out in the open, by the winter garden. If only a swifter predator had finished him off; but she knew that she might have given him too much codeine.

Could this grangeful of rural worthies feel the death or dwindling of species on their own bodies, like a pain around the heart? One hundred and fifteen bobcats ran in the Berk-shires, according to the latest headcount. Inspecting some acreage near Mount Greylock, Marit had come upon one of them. Along for the walk—if mincing in wedge heels was walking—Lola had gone off to see if the real-estate agent had been lying about a trout pool on the property. She had come back to find Marit with a spotted body laid, Pietà fashion, across her lap, the tufted ears and neck ruff drooping limp in death; and Marit holding a spring-trap out before her, which encased one severed, dripping paw, like a reliquary. Lola had stumbled out of her shoes and crouched down. She had dragged and pulled until Marit gave up the trap, and torn off her silk ascot and mopped at the blood on her friend's arms.

"Honey lamb, you're a mess; poor fella; he's not a bob-*kitty*; stop calling him that; Marit, I'm going to have to slap you!"

Marit's mouth twitched, and tears filled her eyes. She wiped them with the tips of her fingers, pretending that she had a lash or a mote caught under her lid, in case anyone was watching her. She preferred to think of herself as a person who did not cry easily. She had not wept at Vlado's deathbed as he lay choking on his last breath. Luba had usurped all the grief in the atmosphere, leaving her daughter dry and stone-faced. Was she weeping now for herself or for the animals? Was their danger only a mirror of her own helplessness? Scorn and dishonor, if she were just a well of self-pity, and the animals her way of plumbing it. Was it merely her own death she saw on the charts that she scanned, the yearly census of diminishing animal populations? She could imagine shooting a woman in a leopard coat, or a dandy in elephant-hide moccasins, with a shell of outsize caliber and without remorse. Did Geronimo scalp white soldiers out of bloodlust, or to defend his shrinking homelands? If there were no wild corners left, the world would be like this unventilated Grange Hall, filled with upright sheep musing quietly in their chairs.

Marit saw a figure—two figures—across the hall, and felt a presence behind her.

"I don't like to disturb you in your private thoughts, Miss Deym."

It was Sheriff Stoeber. She did not bother to turn and acknowledge him. Her gaze was fixed on Gabriel Frankman in the distance. A woman was with him, claiming his attention. She was carrying a schoolbag shaped like a briefcase, or a briefcase that looked like a schoolbag. There was a large percentage of men and boys at Meyerling: had Gabriel vowed never to associate with members of his own sex?

"What can I do for you?" Marit asked, giving the Sheriff her profile. Gabriel's companion had chunky calves and a cap of black hair. She wore ballet slippers and a full skirt puffed out with petticoats. Perhaps she thought she had come to a session of country dancing.

"Folks called in about noises out by your Old Road fence."

The Sheriff had sidled into her line of vision, but Marit did not meet his eyes. She addressed a mole in the center of his forehead.

"What kind of noises?" she asked.

He was holding his hat in his hands and kept turning the brim. She shot a look past his head. The black-haired woman was gone. Gabriel was standing alone.

"Like a dog baying. But these folks said it was different."

"I have a malamute, Sheriff. Sometimes he gets into the sanctuary."

"Well, I heard it was more than one, and they answered each other."

Suddenly, Marit caught the threat in his words. She looked him in the eye and favored him with a smile.

"People are like that, Sheriff. They know I keep animals, so they hang around the fence on a dare, like kids on Halloween. Why don't you refer those calls to me? We must educate people."

She extended her hand and he touched the tips of her fingers. Then she nodded. He took her nod as a dismissal and backed away as if he had been trained, like a courtier, not to turn his back on the sovereign.

Sounds of alarm began to ring in Marit's head, scoring pictures of ruin. Pictures of beautiful cream-gray Lakona and her new wolf pups, ambushed in their den. Pictures of hunters with fresh-killed skins hanging from their belts, wiping their bloody knives across their thighs. Marit made her way toward the rear of the Grange. The anteroom would be empty. She slipped through the inside doors into the entrance hall. No one was there, just a pile of leaflets on a trestle table. She pressed the heels of her palms into her eye sockets, pressed as hard as she could, to wipe out images of doom with a pattern of flashing dots.

She felt hands pulling on her forearms, pulling her hands away from her eyes. She could only see black, but she gave in to Gabriel's touch. Now his hands were linked behind her head, cradling her head, and his voice murmured words to calm horses (*easy, easy, steady there, hold on*), until the fight went out of her shoulders, which were squared all her waking hours.

"I came to find you," he said, and pressed her head down on his shoulder.

She could see now, and remember her dread. She shied away from him.

"You know. You saw them," she said, and for an instant she thought that he might have called the Sheriff.

"What did I see?" he asked, moving a half-step toward her.

"You saw the wolves. The Sheriff knows I have wolves. I need more barbed wire. I can raise the voltage. I need another malamute, a mate for Nikolai. I could tell him they were howling at each other. . . ."

"You're babbling," said Gabriel. "Keep your voice down."

He advanced on her, crowding her. She held up her arms to ward him off. He reached out and wound his hand in her hair, without jerking her head, taking care not to pull her scalp. He raised her head, requiring her to look at him. She was very still, like a cat being held by its scruff.

There was a rumble from behind the inside doors. The meeting was over. Gabriel whipped his arms to his sides as if he had been spined.

"Let's go home," he said, grabbing her hand. She did not stop to question his choice of words. They dashed toward the outside door and made a vaudeville exit. He stubbed one rubber toe on a warped floorboard, while she grappled two-handed with the rusty doorknob that would not turn. He sent the door flying, finally, with a kick from the same stubbed foot, and an angry groan.

Marit drove back to the house with the accelerator down to the floor, as if an all-points bulletin had been put out on her car. Inside the house, she pushed the door shut very carefully in order to damp the faintest clicking of the lock. They crossed the hallway on the tips of their toes and sneaked up the staircase, wincing when they made a stair board creak. Marit led the way over the carpeted corridor toward her childhood bedroom. At the open door of another bedroom Gabriel pulled her back. He pointed inside.

It was Luba's room, converted to a guest room. A galaxy of silver-framed photographs had stood on the bureau and covered the walls; they were stored in the attic now, boxed and tied and labeled. Luba had slung ropes of amethyst, coral, and pearls over the mirror sconces; she thought it was too fussy to coil each necklace up, every time she wore it, in its own chamois case. When she supervised Vilma, her maid, packing for a trip, Luba had a photographic memory of the contents of her drawers and closets, down to the color system by which her sweaters and lingerie were filed. When she came home late from a dinner, and Vilma was asleep, her memory failed her; she let her garments lie wherever she happened to step out of them. She had done her maquillage in the center of the room, without a mirror, smoking and talking to Marit or Vilma. Marit had never crossed the blue Chinese rug without raising clouds of face powder as she walked.

Since Luba's death, Marit had purged the room of its patrician slovenliness, but not its glamour. It was a room that trapped the light and held it, even as the day waned, in the chased surface of the silver altar candlesticks on the dressing table, in the oval mirror framed in gilt-wood ribbons over the headboard, in the golden eyes of the peacock feathers printed on the bedspread and the heavy looped draperies.

"Here," said Gabriel very softly. "It has a double bed."

Marit laughed out loud. "Why are we being so stealthy?"

They moved to the side of the bed, facing each other, their arms crossed in front of their chests. A space of two feet yawned between them. Gabriel's back was to the window. The late-afternoon sun struck him from behind, outlining his figure with light. His features were in shadow; she could not read his face to get her cues. She shut her eyes and reached out a hand to feel his cheek. He turned his face into her palm and kissed it; then he pulled her over the gap.

How much kissing any couple does standing up is a matter of stamina. If they discover that their mouths fit, that their teeth have nerve endings, and that they like quick tongues, their knees will take longer to buckle, but they will fall of their own weight, eventually, on the floor or the bed. If they are wearing light summer clothes and no underwear, the clownish business of undressing is accomplished faster. The man's socks give the only trouble, since removing socks, when he is lying on his back, requires two hands and a sudden forward arching of his body.

The night the wolves brought Gabriel to Marit, they had gone to bed in the dark; the only memory they had of each other's body was lodged in their fingers and on their skins. They could see each other now, the pale one and the dark one, against the background of royal-blue fabric patterned with peacock feathers. They touched what they saw, reviving memories and laying in new ones: Marit's breasts, round and full, but placed high; the line of down that led from Gabriel's navel to his pubic curls. In pubic patches, the spectrum runs from modest to riotous: hers was discreet and close-fitting; his was woolen. They did not break their pace with a long spell of musing and looking. Marit and Gabriel had the same metabolism; they wanted it fast, not slow. They wanted peaks, not erotic bypaths, no stopping and starting, no ice cubes, no garters, no honey and pepper on the lingam, no foreign inserts that play the chorus from Beethoven's Ninth. They paused once, on their knees, to look at themselves in the mirror, whose antique silver backing had worn and reflected them chastely.

Of the act itself, there is never any memory, no more than there is of being stuck at the top of a Ferris wheel, or of the pain of tonsils being cauterized. Some of the stage business is remembered later, and some of the sound cues: Gabriel covered Marit; she did not have to guide him in; they both made a lot of noise; the door to the bathroom was open and a tap was dripping. If Marit had been more experienced, she would have known enough to be grateful to Gabriel for not starting up to soap and rinse his penis. They had not pulled back the covers; there would be crusty white spots on the peacock feathers.

Gabriel collapsed on his back like a sprinter after a race. He did not open his eyes, even to look at her, until he woke up later when the room was nearly dark. Marit curled in as close as she could, on her side, with her head on his shoulder. She was not at peace, but she would not move, or disturb him. She did not know how to nap or doze, so she was consigned to keeping the vigil. Their skins were stuck together. Her arm, which was lying below his belly, had the beginning of a cramp in the wrist. She flexed her hand slowly, but he flinched and murmured. She scanned his face; he seemed to be frowning. He had that look, which she remembered from their first encounter, of a soldier in effigy, alien and complete and locked away, making a lie of their perfect connection. There was no clock in the room, and she could not calculate the time. His features were drawn and sharpened with fatigue; he might sleep for an hour, or through the night. She felt a surge of guilt for her greed, which had drained the spirit from him. How was she going to lie without moving for even an hour, with one arm bent under her like a broken wing? Her other arm, resting on the hair that grew above his penis, had started to itch.

A breeze had blown up outside, as it does in the foot-hills, to chase away the heat of summer afternoons. Their sweat had cooled, and Marit was chilly except where their bodies were touching. There was a lap robe draped over the foot of the chaise longue, if only she could get it. Why was she clinging like a limpet to a reef, alive with discomfort, cut off from grace by the stony form of a sleeping man? She was not the same girl; she had turned into a craven mendi-cant. The world had stopped until he woke up. When he did wake up, they would have to begin from zero. Shared ec-stasy gave her no rights and no expectations; it had wiped out the past and created a void around them. That was not exact: she thought she knew what to expect. He would open his eyes, as dazed as a victim of concussion, search the room for some sign of his location, and stare at her as if she were a stranger. He had said the magic I Love You. He had said it more than once, along with other binding endearments. But his words and caresses were single and separate; they did not build a personal history.

Daughters of Magyars do not lie shivering in the ser-vice of commoners. Marit pulled away from him and scram-bled off the bed, bouncing the mattress and making the bedposts vibrate. She shot a rueful look over her shoulder, but he had not moved. He was dead, for her purposes; he belonged entirely to himself. Her white flannels and blue linen shirt were heaped at her feet—boyish rumpled clothes that usually gave her Dutch courage. His khaki trousers, with a belt through the waist, were piled under hers. Another menial instinct took hold of her. She held up the pants by the cuffs, bringing the creases together so that she could fold them over the chair and hang out the wrinkles. As she folded them, his wallet fell out of the back pocket, with a plonk, on the floor. There are very few girls, newly in love and muddled by it, who would put a billfold full of secrets back in its place, and not stand rooted with alarm like a soldier who knows that he is holding a live grenade. Marit hunkered down out of eyeshot from the bed, bare and trembling, but no longer from the cold.

It was a cheap, battered wallet, coming unsewn, filled with plastic windows. Some still-benign part of her brain remembered a drawerful of Vlado's accessories, among which was an elegant passport-size case of Italian leather. She would give it to Gabriel; she would like to give him beautiful things. There were cards in the windows, nothing to account for her sped-up heartbeat—Social Security, Walker Niles Memorial Library, draft status, blood type, driver's license. Other items were stuffed behind the cards that showed through the plastic. She squeezed apart one of the windows and pulled out a piece of ruled paper, which was written on in a crabbed, miniature script. The paper had been folded many times, and she leaned close to read it: *hooded merganser, scaup, rough-legged hawk, brown creeper, pine siskin, dark-eyed junco....* It was his life-list of birds, with numbers beside the names for the month, day, and year in which he had sighted the species.

She smiled to herself and decided to open the other

windows, in the interest of thoroughness, like a chore to be got out of the way. In the center of the second window was a stiff piece of paper, which stuck. She pulled it out carefully. It was a photograph, in profile, of a girl. Squeezing open the next window, her fingers fumbled. There was something inside. The same girl, full-face and smiling. A girl like an illustration from the fairy books, the kind of girl who turns into trees, wears a train of dewdrops, is borne across the waves on a cockleshell. On the back of the photographs, written in the same tiny script as the life-list, she read "Francesca, Vinalhaven, 1955."

Marit sat down on the floor, crossed her legs, and arched her back. She could hear her heart thudding in half time in her temples. There was no other sound, inside or outside the room, no crickets or tree frogs, no breeze through the leaves, no owl or animal cries, or cars on the road. She was as still as the world around her, calm and suspended, like the landscape when a tornado is in the neighborhood. She felt no pain as she had at the fair. Gabriel's student seemed like a figment of a rival; the fairy creature in the snapshot was a fact of his secret life. Marit felt poised and excited, as if she had always known that this girl existed, or someone like her. Her eyesight was as clear as her brain, and she scanned the darkening room like a hunting cat.

Gabriel was sitting up. He held out his arms to her.

"I had a bad dream," he said. "You went away."

She saw how frail and unguarded he looked. He had slept his hair into cowlicks. The wallet was still in her hands. There was no way to hide it.

"You weren't dreaming," she answered. "I got out of bed because I was cold and got right into trouble."

He reached over to the bedside table and turned on the lamp. She held up the wallet.

"It fell out of your pants," she said, "but I didn't have to open it."

"Open it, baby, open it. I'm yours, it's yours, what's the problem?"

Marit hung her head. "Perhaps you should have told me."

"Told you what? How much time have we had for talking?"

She could not look him in the face. She was losing bravado like an airplane losing altitude.

"The pictures." She paused for a second, waiting for the sword to fall. "Snapshots," she said, bearing down hard on both parts of the word. It was taking Gabriel a long time to react. It had already taken him six or seven seconds. When she was swimming underwater, she could only hold her breath for a count of ten.

Now he was down on the floor in front of her, so nimble and goatlike that she had not heard him climb off the bed. He leaned over to kiss her shoulder, just above her breast. She reached out and cupped his soft penis, forgetting that she had no rights, that her head was on the block for committing Pandora's crime. He took the wallet away from her and opened it. She had not filed the full-face snapshot, which floated down on the rug.

"My poor Francesca." He shook his head. "We were going to be married. I killed her."

Marit shifted her position. There was a note of piety in his voice that made her restless. He clasped his hands in his lap and lifted up his eyes, like old paintings of St. Peter Martyr with the axe through his skull.

"I blew up at her," Gabriel recited, "about a piece of nonsense. She ran out of the house in front of a truck. She is buried at Matlock. I go there to see her. For a while I used to go there twice a week."

Marit reached for her shirt, in case it could give her some protection. She pulled it on.

"I have a black temper," Gabriel challenged her. "My temper killed her."

Marit stood up and backed away to the window, pulling her shirttails together to cover her groin.

"Now she's your life's work." Marit faced him with her chin up. "Is that what you're telling me?"

Gabriel frowned. He did not unclasp his hands.

"It gives your life a shape," said Marit, "mourning and repenting."

He drew his knees in close to his chest and dug his clasped knuckles into his forehead.

"I want to be rid of her," he said. "She clings to me. She wants to take me with her."

"You adore it." Marit showed her teeth. "You're a living shrine."

Gabriel lay back on the floor, one arm covering his face. When he spoke he sounded sad and far away.

"How hard your voice is."

Marit took criticism badly, especially when it was justified. It is truer to say that she took any comment on her actions, however apt, and heard it as criticism. When she was stung, she raised the ante and fought like an animal. In another century she would have whipped her critic for lèse majesté. The process was circular: in the end it was herself she was punishing, hating herself more than she hated her

I I I

critic, so that there was no way out but weeping and groveling and prostration.

"I see. I've nicked your plaster saint. I've tracked mud into the shrine." She could not stop. Her nostrils began to prickle, an early warning of tears.

He propped himself up on his elbows and looked at her with calm, mild eyes. His nakedness was noble and candid, and gave him the advantage over her.

"I told you something that I am ashamed of. I wanted your help. Instead you are jealous of a dead girl."

"I'm jealous, all right." Marit was all precarious swagger. "I'd like to uproot her and scatter her."

"Jealousy is a demeaning emotion. It is a waste of energy for a spirit like yours."

Marit felt a knot forming under her rib cage. She had gone too far. His lofty tone was a sign that he had hardened his heart against her. A wave of grief or sickness made her dizzy. She slid to the floor and tried to meet his eyes. He was smoothing the young girl's photograph between his palms, as if Marit's touch had wrinkled and bent the paper.

Marit had never asked for pardon since her childhood, and her lips would not pronounce the simple formula. She said his name and waited for an answer. She spoke again, "Please, Gabriel"; and once more, "Please . . ."

He looked at her with courteous disinterest, like a doctor who has squeezed an ailing patient into a schedule that was already overcrowded.

"Please talk to me. I have to hear. What was she like?" Marit pressed her back against the wall to brace herself for what he might disclose.

"She was gentle and frail." He studied the picture. He

spoke like someone who is thinking aloud. "She forgot to eat. I had to feed her. I cut the pieces of food very small, or she couldn't swallow. I gave her drinks made with eggs and she sipped them from a spoon."

"Was she ill?" Marit kept her voice steady by biting her lip.

"She was ill as a child. I think she had rheumatic fever. She missed a year of school, but she read so much that they put her two grades ahead."

"A prodigy," said Marit, whose lower lip was taking a beating. Gabriel stared into the middle distance. He had not heard her.

"She was so small. It was caused by the fever. Her hands were tiny. She had boneless little feet. I came home with a colleague one night and he saw her boots drying outside the door. 'I didn't know you had children,' he said. That was one of our jokes."

It did not sound funny to Marit, who was trying to take her punishment like a man. She did not question the fitness of her ordeal. If Hell had ten circles, instead of only nine, the tenth would be reserved for the jealous, who must listen, until the trump sounded, to the voice of their lovers extolling the merits of a rival.

Gabriel turned to Marit, but his eyes were fixed and dull. If she left the room, he would have gone on talking, in a voice that was as flat as his gaze, a voice more suited to confessing sins than to singing praises.

"She had no one else to take care of her. Her father was old, the age of a grandfather. Her mother was dead. She was a late-life child. Late-life children are usually gifted, like Francesca."

Marit tasted blood. She had bitten her lip open. She

ground her back teeth together to keep from venting her hatred of the frail, small, late-life child. She feared that Gabriel would see her jaws working, and, in fact, he was watching her now, as if he were observing a sample of tissue under a microscope to find out if the cells were healthy or diseased. He was testing her, trying to provoke another jealous lapse, proving her worth by putting her through fire. The heat of jealousy was easier to bear than the fact that he had named himself her censor.

He looked her straight in the eye and went on talking, rolling over her pain like a mower over grass, which cuts down frogs and insects as well as plants, specks of life which are invisible from the mower's height.

"I loved her because she lived inside her head. She drew pictures of Persian princes hunting tigers. She thought that the outside world was like those pictures. . . ."

Marit gave up fighting. She knew from her terms in school that every test is rigged against the candidate.

"You're lying. You didn't love her. You were her nursemaid."

Gabriel smiled. She thought he smiled with satisfaction. She had failed the test, just as he had predicted.

"That was part of it. I signed on for it. I also loved her."

"You liked being stronger. You wanted to keep her weak."

Gabriel refused to engage with Marit at her level. "I would be lying if I pretended I didn't love her."

Marit bowed her head. "You're still in love with her."

"Who are you hurting by twisting my words? You're hurting yourself."

"I heard you say it. You said you loved her."

Gabriel stood up and pulled on his trousers. He looked down at Marit.

"I come with a past. I'm stuck with my past the way I'm stuck with being short. If you want me, you take the whole package."

"You don't want me. You're leaving."

"Why should I hang around? This is your scenario and I don't know the lines."

"I've had my last chance. I'm expunged from the moral record." Marit's mouth was working wildly. She was trying to talk over sobs.

"Then you've expunged yourself. I'm not going to take that rap."

"You're condemning me." Marit covered her face with her hands. "You have your rules and I've broken all of them." Her fingers were working as if she could tear her flesh.

Gabriel was dressed. He began to pick up her clothes.

"I love you. I don't love your behavior."

"They're the same god-damned thing!"

"You have your behavior, but you are not your behavior."

"You're talking Chinese." The words came out like a hiccup, or a question, with a note of hope behind them, as if she had discovered the thread in the labyrinth.

He sat on the bed with his feet on the floor and his hands on his knees, tranquil and untouchable. If he had been an elderly person, he would have steepled his fingers.

"You're going to have to get used to the fact that I am not judgmental. If I love you, I approve you unconditionally."

"Then you should also approve my behavior." Marit was petitioning, but she could not help it.

"I love you for what you are. Your actions are ephemeral."

She felt ragged and hot and grimy. Because of the strife or the pious conundrums, she was getting a headache. Her uncombed hair and her dirty knees might be ephemeral, but they were all, for the moment, that he could see of her; therefore they were her. Her inner light would not iron her shirt or wash her feet. It seemed to her that what Gabriel wanted was perfection, that her surface should always reflect her essence, and that her inside always illuminate her outside.

"You need to be alone," he said.

"Don't tell me what I need if you're going to leave me."

He went over to her and kissed her on the forehead, a pastoral kiss of love and absolution.

"I can't put you back on course. You have to do that for yourself."

He walked to the bedroom door and smiled back from the sill.

"I'm your good girl," she called.

He did not answer. She heard him pad down the hall in his sneakers. She heard him jog down the stairs. He was hurrying to be gone. He was tripping down the drive, as free as air, leaving her hunched and smarting, like Caliban under Prospero's censure.

If she believed in his unconditional love, she would be a dupe. Life is a court; the trial lasts a lifetime; the jury sits in perpetuity. Every person is a machine adding up grievances and faults and ticking away. When the machine reaches fault one thousand, or one hundred thousand, or any number, love is cut off, automatically and forever. If Gabriel maintained that he was non-judgmental, he was imitating God. All that any humble person should say is that he is less judgmental than other people, that you can commit more errors in his presence without forfeiting his love than you can in the presence of someone else. Since Gabriel was not God, the number of free faults that he would allow was finite. If she committed one error over his free-fault capacity, her head would come off, she would burn, she would hang, like the lowest of criminals.

A dog barked and kept on barking, drawing Marit out of her thoughts. It was Nikolai, trying to tell her that he was hungry. Gabriel had put her slacks on the chair, but she had to grope under the bed for her sandals. There was one lamp burning in Luba's room. The rest of the rooms were dark. She went downstairs to turn on the lights and reclaim the house.

SIX

Luba Deym had never read aloud to her daughter at bedtime. She had told her stories instead, which began while Marit was undressing, continued through her bath and teeth-brushing, and went on after she was tucked under the covers, with the lights out. There were no ducks, beavers, bears, or orphans in Luba's repertory, so Marit had been raised on were-beasts, enchanted suits of armor and heath wraiths. These spectral friends were some of Marit's favorites, as was the child-vampire, but the stories that she liked best belonged to the buried-alive cycle, which Luba had heard at the feet of her own grandmother, Pàla, when she was a child herself, in Hungary.

Luba's accounts of being buried alive started with someone waking up in a very tight space, raising his arms or lifting his head, and striking a solid barrier, which was then perceived as wood or metal and followed by the instantaneous recognition that he was in a coffin. Then came the horrific shrieks, the banging of the fists on the lid, the bloodying of the fists from much banging on the wood, the calculation of the air supply, and the gasping and heaving from the anticipation of smothering.

Then Luba would switch the viewpoint: she moved outside the coffin, to the dark nave of a church or a side chapel; to a parlor where the coffin stands in the center of the rug, banked by waxy flowers; or to the cemetery where fresh earth shows the outline of the grave and no headstone has yet been planted. In the church an ancient sacristan makes his rounds. He is partially deaf, so he cannot hear the noises until he passes by the candlelit Lady chapel. Fists banging sound like mice scrabbling to his ears, but his attention is fixed by the lid of the coffin being raised, just inches, and falling to. The prisoner within is too weak to throw the lid aside. The sacristan is terrified, suspects a supernatural incident, and stumbles out to wake the vicar. (In some versions Luba's sacristan was not only deaf but drunk, and went back to his pile of blankets in the crypt to drink himself from delirium to oblivion.)

In the mansion containing the lying-in-state parlor, the children's governess wakes from a nightmare, and for precious minutes thinks that the muffled screams she hears are a continuation of the dream. Or the overweight housemaid has crept down to the kitchen, lured by a cold meat pie, and is cutting very thin slices so that no one will notice the theft. Five thin slices add up to one thick one, however, and the cook has an eagle eye. With the fifth slice halfway to her mouth, the housemaid hears moans coming from the parlor and drops the pie onto the floor, to incriminate her forever.

In the cemetery, the cries from the coffin alternate with owls hooting, and no human hears them, unless Luba introduced a pair of adventurous lovers into the story. What the grave-robber would see if the coffin lid was not nailed down securely is a white forearm reaching through the dirt, with fingers splayed and bloody. The frightened lovers might run to the local constabulary, or they might not. If the constable, who has been dragged away from a nap in his desk chair, arrives at the grave before its inhabitant chokes to death on a mouthful of crumbly earth, he will only be able to effect a partial rescue: his Lazarus will be alive, but raving.

Luba was the queen of fireside storytellers, but she was not, by American standards, a fit mother. She felt that children enjoyed being frightened, that it enlivened their imaginations and gave them a healthy respect for the unknown. To give her credit, Luba took care to ground her tales in reality. Before medicine was a science, she would explain, doctors could not tell if a person was dead or only in coma. If the corpse woke up and tried to struggle out of his grave, peasants (never noblemen, to Marit's recollection) would cry out that the dead were walking. Premature burial, in Luba's theory, was the origin of vampires, zombies, and ghouls. Marit had memorized the names and traits of the undead before she learned to recite the kings of England and France. She begged her mother to tell her more stories; she also begged for a night-light.

Perhaps Luba had run out of stories, or perhaps she was tired of embroidering the old tales over and over again. One night she brought out a new one, but she claimed that it was factual. Marit was nine years old, and Luba may have thought she had grown unshockable. Luba was a performer as well as a storyteller, and Marit was not just her child, but her audience. Lately Marit had been scratching and yawning during the story, and Luba searched her mind for ways to refurbish her repertory. Nothing excuses the story she then told, or the harm that it did. The story was about Marit herself, and it had happened in the Windward Islands. Marit could not remember a trip to the islands, though she had seen pictures of herself as a smaller child on a broad white beach.

When Marit was three, according to Luba, they had gone to Bacou, in the Grenadines. Vlado had started work on a new invention, so he stayed behind. He had drawn preliminary sketches for the automatic cigarette smoker: an ashtray designed to light a cigarette, advance it on a metal arm to the smoker's lips at measured intervals, then incinerate the fag end so that no ash was left, just a fine white dust. When his wife and daughter sailed, he was failing to solve the problem of the self-incinerator.

One day Marit had come up to her mother, who was oiling herself on the beach. "A red bee bit me," she had said, chattering with fever, and held out her swollen left wrist to show her the bite. The best balm for bee-sting is a paste of bicarbonate of soda, and Luba had applied it to the hardened swelling. No ordinary insect had bitten Marit, for within an hour her fever had risen to one hundred and five, and the paste on her wrist had flaked off from the burning heat. After the fever had come delirium, after delirium unconsciousness, after coma the cessation of all life signs—a process so formal and inferential that Death might have been a logician demonstrating a theorem on the blackboard for his slowest pupil.

Death's interest in Marit was only theoretical, but his pupil had a literal turn of mind. The medical eminence on Bacou was Dr. Iñiguez, the hotelkeeper, who had left an unaccredited dental practice on the Venezuelan mainland to cash in on the tourist business. Dr. Iñiguez, with hair in his ears and warty thumbs, was enraptured by Marit's case: "*No hay duda, Madang Deng, Marita está con los ángeles.*" Why he did not doubt that she was with the angels when her cheeks still flushed pink and her limbs remained un-stiffened, Luba never questioned. She was in a walking coma herself and could not speak to give instructions. Iñiguez wired to Union Island on the Coast Guard radio, not for medical corroboration, but for a priest.

"*Tenemos que encajonarla, Madang,*" worried Dr. Iñiguez. Since there was no ready-made coffin to embox her, to protect her from insects and larger meat-eaters, they laid her in Luba's lacquered steamer trunk, on a bed of the rose tissue paper that Vilma had packed with. "*Parece una muñeca,*" wept Mrs. Iñiguez. After taking Luba to her room, Mrs. Iñiguez dressed Marit in white, fluffed out her hair, and dabbed a touch of carmine on her lips, so that she looked more like a doll than ever.

For years Marit had had one recurring nightmare, which she dreamed at irregular, if longer, intervals. As she fought her way out of the dream, it seemed hours before she realized that her fists were hammering on her own patchwork quilt, which had crawled up over her head, that her elbows, jerking sideways uncontrollably, were striking the tightly tucked sheets of her cot-width bed, not the wooden sides of Luba's lacquered footlocker. Marit knew from Luba's story that

Mrs. Iñiguez had kept a vigil, and had been mesmerized to sleep in her chair by the flickering of the candles which she had set on every surface and sill in the room. How could she, Marit, have been screaming for more than ten seconds before Mrs. Iñiguez had tripped the locks and saved her, keening and crying *"Es un milagro* [It is a miracle]"?

After one of these dreams Marit slept badly and woke often. She never slept well, and she rarely slept through the night. When she woke, she could not go back to sleep until she made a patrol. Tonight she had waked up five times and done five patrols cellar to attic, making her rounds in a kind of stupor, like a wind-up night watchman. She did not have to carry a lantern or wield a flashlight; she kept all the lights burning downstairs and a burglar-tease lit in one of the attic storerooms. She hardly knew, anymore, if it was supernatural or human assault that she was patrolling against, and she no longer got down to look under the beds, although she stalked the floor-length velvet draperies in the living room, and had been known to lean her ear against them before giving them a cautionary jerk. Sometimes she grew bored and impatient, and longed to throw off the need to patrol. At other times she found things undone or amiss, which made her compulsive rounds imperative: tonight the front door was not on the chain, and the kitchen window had been latched on a vulnerable diagonal instead of being pushed down firmly in its groove.

Marit had begun to patrol after her parents had died, when she was living alone. At first her rounds had a ritual quality, like superstition, an attempt to placate the gods or the fates or the shades, no different from sprinkling lamb's blood on a local altar, or laying the first fruits of the harvest at a crossroads. Soon her ritual acts had hardened into the fixed behavior of phobia, as it was bound to, since Marit had been phobic from childhood onward in little ways. Phobia spreads through the psyche like a cold fog; it alters the cell structure. Lop off one of its heads, and up rears another: in Marit's childhood gallery of phobias, praying mantises had given way to snail slime; hairs in food had been succeeded by amputees; Aztec sacrifice had been replaced by birds loose in rooms. Now phobia was a natural condition, a genetic fact like her gray-green eyes, square jaw, and spatulate fingertips. She found it easy enough to adjust to phobia. It simply meant that she lived at the ready, like a fighter for the sound of the bell. She had learned to think of life as a minefield.

The mine that she was skirting this morning—an overcast morning with the light no stronger at ten o'clock than it had been at dawn—was the image of Gabriel retreating the night before. Every word out of her mouth had quickened his pace down the staircase and out the drive, and hastened his way home to his monklike room, where he might have taken the forgotten picture of Francesca out of his wallet and propped it against the lamp on his desk; or wedged it into the corner of the mirror; or made a note to have it enlarged and buy a frame for it. It occurred to Marit that jealousy had a boomerang effect: it could revive the cult of the rival. Her jealous scene had brought Francesca back to life.

Marit was an apprentice to the effects of jealousy, but now she knew, without experience to teach her, that a jealous person must grind her teeth and wear a mask. Jealousy is an affliction to be hidden, repressed, covered up, and lied about, like a mysterious ulcerated sore that could be the beginning of leprosy. Otherwise the lover will shrink away, gathering his robes around him for fear of contamination, and withdraw from the afflicted person, for whom there is no cure except lifelong quarantine. Last night Marit had seen that fear of infection cross Gabriel's face, a puzzled look, as if he could not identify the source of a fecal smell. She wanted to hate him for his fastidiousness and purity, for his work with the holy blind, whose affliction does not mar their physical surface. She wanted to condemn him to work in the dangerous wards of a madhouse, and watch the disintegration of his charity. The mad, in their rages, know that they are ugly and unlovable; still they want to be loved and redeemed. So does the jealous person. But their keepers or lovers are never equal to the task. They would requisition the equipment of animal tamers, if it were allowed, to handle their charges—thick quilted gloves, a pointed stick, and a buggy whip.

A draught of jealousy is the quickest shrinking-potion in the emotional pharmacy. Marit felt evil and lowered, reduced to the status of a rabid gnome. Her gender was threatened; any moment she might start hopping and spitting. Or tear the telephone out of the wall, since it refused to ring. She had never waited for calls or letters from boys or men. She had never been one-down, in Dutch, or on the hook. Gabriel's disfavor was hives, boils, splinters, and fleabite; there was no salve for such a rash, except for murder.

At eleven-thirty she started pinching back the house plants. She went through the coleus, the saxifrage, the eyelash begonia, and the wandering Jew. She had bitten her nails short and uneven, so that there was no deft, clean severing of the leaves, more a matter of squash and tear, leaving the stems bleeding green. Mounds of raped foliage lay around the four pots. She pruned plants like a plague of locusts, according to Lola. Marit eyed the pepper elder. She was not appeased, and one more runty plant would not appease her.

At one o'clock a group of children from the Meyerling Community were coming to release the airlifted animals into the sanctuary. This was a sham adventure, like all the excursions that Henry Dufton planned for them. After inspecting the metal carriers to make sure that the airholes were placed far away from the handles, and that small fingers were safe from claws and darting fangs, Mr. Dufton had agreed to let the children carry the cages just inside the sanctuary, onto the wide strip of land that had been cleared to keep the animals from approaching the fence. Then three of the counselors would take the cages a short way into the woods, open the hatches, and set the trapped animals free. Miss Fellowes would stay behind with the children and give them a nature talk. Marit had heard one of her talks at a Meyerling parents' weekend. Miss Fellowes reduced the creatures of the wild to toyshop scale: bears were "woolly"; hares were "downy" and "flop-eared"; and raccoons were always referred to as "little bandits." If sight was ever restored to her blind listeners, Marit thought, they would have trouble telling a real animal from a stuffed one, and pay for their confusion with one or both of their new eyes.

George Schulte had already delivered the animals in their cages. Marit had heard his truck while she was working on the house plants, and had watched him take down the box traps and line them up in even rows by the garage. The creatures inside the traps had not stirred. They were dopey from their ride in the truck and the helicopter, and from being loaded and unloaded so many times during the last few days. Marit wondered if the price of their rescue would be a shortened life span. She would be able to tell, since they were banded, except for the snake, and she had the list of band numbers for her records.

Marit had arranged her day so that this outing did not require her participation, but it made claims on her attention all the same. She forced herself to ask the young blind for walks or picnics, or special events like this animal-releasing. She made plans with the Community on the telephone: the sanctuary key and map of safe open territory were in the mailbox; there were two bathrooms on the lower floor; there would be milk and soda in the refrigerator. These arrangements satisfied her debt to form and kindness, allowing her to leave the house and stay away until the children were gone.

This afternoon Marit did not leave the house. She hid, instead, in the empty butler's apartment over the garage, standing back from the window in order to prevent being seen and waved down. She hid to indulge her wary, angry pity, and made herself watch to acquit her wretched weakness.

She spied now on the docile covey assembled in the courtyard below, sixteen children dressed in their camp uniforms—Alpine walking shorts, high snake-boots, and crimson wind-jackets. They stood waiting for instructions from the counselors, wearing the corners of their mouths upturned like smiles. Those upbeamed mouths were as much a badge of blindness as white canes for city blind. Was it the sweet, wrenching smile of souls in grace, or a facial set molded by the habit and bond of dependency? Marit tried to see them, this time, as normal, boisterous children. She studied them carefully to see if anybody was pinching anybody else's arm, or kicking the gravel, if one of the boys was sticking chewing gum in the hair of one of the girls, if any child talked too loud or tried to leave the group. They just waited, as passive as clay, turning their heads in the direction of the noise when a car door slammed, pressing closer together when Nikolai began to bark from his pen on the far side of the house.

At the top of the driveway Marit could see the hood of the limousine that had brought them, one of a fleet of four—two black, and two liturgical maroon—that Bishop Meyerling had acquired during his term of office. When he died, the Bishop had left an endowment to keep up the fleet, with a provision in his will for a mechanic as curator. Four counselors were bringing blankets and lunch baskets up from the limousines. Marit knew Miss Fellowes, who ran the sports program during the school term and the camp during the summer. Miss Fellowes was an innovator; she had had the sides of the swimming pool padded in foam rubber, so that blind swimmers could have races without striking their heads at the end of a lap. With the help of two young men with whistles on loops around their necks, Miss Fellowes was standing pairs of children—boy-girl, boy-girl—at either side of the animal traps, telling them to lift the cages and balance them between them: "Steady, Beverly, it's a skunk, you'll be sorry!" "That's a fox, John and Phyllis, a cunning fox!"

The fourth counselor was down on her knees counting the contents of one of the picnic baskets. She pulled the kerchief off her head and wiped her brow with it, feeling the heat. Her hair was black and caplike and shiny. Marit recognized her as the woman who had come with Gabriel to the Airlift meeting, and she straightened up from her shrinking position at the window with a red jolt of dislike.

Miss Fellowes was moving the group out now, using the bullhorn: "Single file, boys and girls, slow march! Short grass all the way; no cow-flops!" One girl, with breasts, and taller than the others, turned around to face Marit's window directly. Marit fell back as if the gaze were a sniper's bullet. The girl's eyes looked like live eyes, with no whitish over-cast, slanted like a tiger's, with low-slung lids. She smiled up at the window, a live smile, with too much gum showing, holding her breasts high, precocious and aware of her body. *Why is she posing? They are clairvoyant; she knows I'm here*—Marit's heart was beating as if she had been found out. She collected herself and inched forward to take a new look. It was the other one. It was the girl student she had seen at the fair taking a reading lesson with Gabriel by the tennis courts. It was Gabriel's whole harem, except for the dead one, smug in her grave, who still worked Gabriel's strings as expertly as she had in life. The inside of Marit's head was fire and mayhem. She wanted revenge, but her enemy was bones and hair, bright hair that took so long to rot, that could outlast flesh and bone and winding-cloth.

It took a tug on the arm by Miss Fellowes to get Gabriel's student back in place by the weasel's cage. "Get a wiggle on, Aimée! Pick up your feet now, boys and girls, we're on a mission!"

If it were Tuesday, Mrs. Paul Gilliam would be at home with her bridge club, and Lola would be on duty making Charleston Devils and watercress sandwiches for the ladies, because Tuesday was the cook's half-day off. Since it was Thursday, Mrs. Gilliam was playing cards at the golf club. Lola might be at home in her suite, which had a separate driveway, or she might be down in Pittsfield. If she was not at home, Marit would have to go without her. Lola had a new flirt in Pittsfield, or nearby, but she refused to tell Marit what her name was. ("Either it's the mayor's wife or she's not a consenting adult." "I'm superstitious; I'm not going to tell you until I've got the case locked up.") In organizing her love affairs, Lola was as discreet as any adulterer whose father-in-law is the president of the corporation. Lola found her women out of town, and never gave them her address or telephone number. She used Virginia Taft as her nom de guerre. ("Who the hell was Virginia Taft?" "She was my only failure; I'll tell you the whole story when we're old ladies.")

Lola worked underground, but the way she worked was risky. The girls she chose were young and virginal, because she liked to do the initiating. Nuns at convent schools like to spy out an early vocation for the same reason: an untainted girl is less likely to have regrets. Young converts, sapphic or religious, can also lapse early, as soon as they are out of their teens. Lola, unlike the Church, had usually finished with them by then. Young girls bored her, for any other than sexual purposes; they were apt to have thoughts and opinions, and want to air them. Lola was cautious about covering her tracks, and she made her choices carefully. She got no credit from Marit for discrimination, because Lola was class-conscious. There had been certain manicurists and certain waitresses, but the girls that Lola wanted most were the snub blonde ones, the ones with unformed noses and short upper lips, with long taut legs and little lines at the corners of their eyes from squinting across the tennis court in the noon sun. The way to these girls was through their tomboy hearts, and Lola had made a lot of time adjusting a stirrup, or teaching awkward fingers how to tie a bass fly.

Marit pulled up in the jeep. She honked the horn once, then twice again, and jumped down, leaving the engine on and the door flapping open. She ran up the outside staircase and tried the door of Lola's apartment. Lola was opening the door at the same time, and Marit tripped as she crossed the sill. Lola caught her by the elbow and laughed at her.

"Hey there, honey doll, you sure have a head of steam up!"

Marit checked herself before she spoke. When Lola talked Southern, it could mean that they were not alone. Then she saw Horty Waite sitting in the chair by the garden window. Horty had an embroidery frame on her lap. She waved at Marit and stitched her needle into the fabric to keep from dropping it.

"I've been helping Mrs. Waite with a crewel pillow," said Lola.

"Oh, it's all lumpy," said Horty. "I'll probably have to throw it on the heap pile."

Marit tried to catch Lola's eye, but Lola had sense enough to look away and go over to Horty. She took the frame out of her hands and examined it.

"It's stretching out just fine, don't you worry."

"Who is it for, Horty?" asked Marit. She was beginning to lose hope of getting Lola away.

Horty lowered her eyes apologetically. "I'm going to put my heart in my throat and give it to Howard's mother. Do you think I dare, Lola? She needlepoints hassocks for the National Cathedral."

Lola made comforting sounds and patted Horty's hand. Marit had a low threshold for girlish dither, and she suspected Lola of egging Horty on. Marit and Lola had an understanding, if not a contract; they gave each other priority over other people. Marit expected Lola to know what was in her head as soon as she knew it; it was one of their private myths that they had a shared brain. Marit knew she was not good at self-inhibition; no one had ever said to her, after a crisis, "You had a fever of one hundred and four? A dying mother? A severed limb? I would never have known it." Marit imagined herself now, seen from the outside, as a walking lightboard, with signals of pain, desperation, and anger winking on and off, fizzing and exploding. And Lola, who knew their agreement, who had helped to write it, was as bland and heedless as if Marit had stopped by to return a book. From what she was about to do Marit needed Lola's protection; she needed opposition from Lola as much as she needed allegiance. She decided to raise her voice and make her claim.

She stood at the top of the steps that led down to the sunken living room.

"We had a date to drive over to Matlock. I can't be late. We can drop Horty at home on the way. You don't mind, Horty, do you?"

Matlock lay five miles northeast of Niles and fifteen miles below the Vermont border. Settled in 1712, it had been wiped out twice before the Revolution by Nipmuck Indians, but this was not the reason that it did not appear on most modern road maps. Matlock had been a mountain retreat for rich Bostonians during the eighteen-eighties; they had left behind several sprawling wooden hotels, and the little Norman chapel of All Souls. The drive from Niles to Matlock was a slow one, on winding back roads that sightseers and tourists rarely used. Marit was driving and Lola had her feet propped up on the dashboard. Every now and then she took a sideways look at Marit, who had covered her bloodshot eyes with wire-rimmed sunglasses.

"I hear you talk about that fellow," said Lola, breaking a long silence, "and I thank God I'm not the straight one."

"I thought you had a code," said Marit. "I thought you only messed with baby girls."

"But Horty is so unhatched. I sometimes think she had those children in her sleep."

"Have you waked her up with a kiss yet?"

"The idea just took me this afternoon. About the time you barged in, old lady."

"You're a cad, Lola. What about Pittsfield?"

"She's cooking, honey, she's cooking. I got a letter from her this morning: 'Dearest V., What must you think of me?' I'll wait a week and then answer it."

"You're pleased with yourself, aren't you? She's sweating and she's off balance and you're flexing your muscles."

"Watch the road!" Lola reached for the wheel. The jeep had swerved over onto the shoulder. "If you're so wrought up, you shouldn't be driving."

They passed a sign, Matlock two miles, lettered on a wooden arrow that pointed straight up at the sky. Lola sat forward, her feet planted flat on the floor, steering and braking along with Marit.

"Would it cost you a lot to obey the speed limit?"

"Get off me, Lola, or I'll drive with my thumbs."

"I am a gem. I jump when you say jump. I don't even ask questions."

"That's right. Don't ask questions."

"Oh, no. You've turned me into a nanny. My role is to nag and scold. I want to know why you're driving to Matlock like an ambulance. You've never been to Matlock in your life."

"Not true. It's the direct route to Bad Mountain."

"You don't ski. You hate to ski."

"I used to ski. Luba made me learn skiing and tennis."

"I'm waiting," said Lola, "and I want a sensible answer."

Marit pushed up her sunglasses and rubbed the bridge of her nose.

"You won't get one from me. All the sense has flown out of my head."

"Leeched out by that runt, no doubt."

"He kept pushing my face in it, Lolly. I had to hear about her hands and her feet, and her adorable habits and her artwork. He kept saying how gifted she was. She was too fine to live. . . ."

"Well, I'm not," snapped Lola. "I have a lot of good years in me yet. Stay in your lane or pull over and let me drive."

Marit took off her glasses and dropped them in Lola's lap.

"Wipe these off for me, please. I smudged them."

"You don't need them. It's your eyes that are bleary. You need a new beau."

"I'm not little and soft. I'm a lout. I've got biceps that show through my sleeves. You've known me three years. Have I even been sick for a day?"

Lola could not find an answer. Her stock of retorts was running out. Marit was talking to herself, or to someone inside her head.

"I looked at myself this morning. The red spots are back. The broken blood vessels. Luba's skin doctor took them off with an electric needle. I spent my youth in that office. There was always something wrong. I had warts, I had spreading moles, I had cysts on my scalp. . . ."

"Marit Deym." Lola slapped the seat. "I will give you to a count of ten to stop this raving."

"Lola?" Marit's voice was shaky. "Do you think that my eyes are set too wide apart?"

Lola reached behind Marit and pushed down the button that locked the door. She locked her own side with her elbow. When Marit had one of her electrical storms, as Lola had named them, Lola depended on feisty talk to bring her around, the kind of talk used with good results by coaches and trainers. Marit preferred a rough harangue to gentle treatment, since she thought that most girls were tender, meeching sissies. Her erratic driving troubled Lola less than hearing her compare herself to one of these weaker specimens, and come out losing. Lola decided to drop the role of master sergeant; she could not shame Marit out of her affliction. Any good sergeant has to change his tone of voice when one of his men has broken under fire.

The road was lined with a screen of foreign poplars. At the next right turn, the line of trees continued, broken fifty yards in by a high, arched iron gate. Marit went past the gate and drove across the road into a fallow field. She parked the jeep behind a stand of wild thorns, out of sight of the road. She jumped out of the jeep and headed for the gate without waiting for Lola.

The iron gate was hanging ajar. It had rusted open. Marit pulled it closed with both hands, as tightly as it could shut, scraping away a sill of earth that had mounded up at the bottom. In front of them stood the chapel, down a lane of boxwood. The box had grown into the lane, forcing them to walk sideways in some places. The chapel was hung with ivy, browned out from lack of pruning, hairy branches of ivy dangling loose and withering off. Inside, the chapel was dark, like a fortress, not a church, with slits, set high near the roof, instead of windows. The altar and the crucifix were shrouded. Three white paste florist's vases stood at the base of the pulpit; one of the vases had toppled over and broken into large pieces.

Marit led the way down the center aisle, holding on to the backs of the pews. A large bird flapped over their heads, the noise of its wings magnified in that empty space. Startled, Marit covered her head and cried out, backing up a few steps and knocking into Lola, who was set on a forward course and pushed Marit onward. They ran out in a welter of sound, footsteps echoing on the tiles, bird squalling and flapping through the nave, and the broken doorknob turning with a fun-house creak.

They stopped running when they reached the little graveyard, which was surrounded by a low picket fence with slats missing, like empty spaces in a row of teeth. The fence was low enough to step over easily, but Lola balked. She waved at Marit, who did not see her. Marit was walking from stone to stone, bending down to look at the inscriptions, which were hard to read because the graveyard lay in dappled shade. The ground was uneven and damp, since the sun never dried it out, and the thin, flat stones all tilted at different angles. Most of the stones were slick with green moss, and some had sunk into the earth above the date line. Marit stepped on patches of ground-cover mint and camomile as she walked, raising gusts of fragrance. There was no smell of death in the graveyard, just the charm of ruin.

One stone stood apart from the others and tilted less, set back in a corner by the fence, in full shadow, under the tallest cedars. Marit squatted down to read the engraving. The marble facing had started to crumble at the edges, but the words were deeply incised and caught the light:

> A Heart Within Whose Sacred Cell
> The Peaceful Virtues Loved to Dwell
> > Francesca Alba Hadley
> > (1932–1955)

Lola stayed outside the fence, keeping watch, rotating her head from Marit to the side door of the chapel and back to Marit, getting an ache in her neck and wishing that she had two heads. Lola was unconcerned about graveyards and mortality; she had spent the night in an empty plantation house that was believed to be haunted by astral cats. Lola was afraid of nothing that bit, crawled, moaned, hurled crockery, or rattled its chains, but she was afraid of Marit's actions, and their meaning.

Marit's mouth was moving; she was making fists and gesticulating, and Lola was too far away to hear the words that the gestures punctuated. Lola stepped back to watch the chapel, peering up and down the line of poplars. She brought her eyes back to Marit again. Marit was kicking a gravestone. Lola stepped over the fence, but still she hung back. Marit picked up a rock and threw it at the headstone. Chips of limestone sprayed over the ground.

Lola thought that she might have to subdue her, though Marit was stronger, and as tall as she was. There was danger in trying to subdue an excessive person. Lola had grappled with an epileptic once and had her hand bitten hard before she could find the tongue. Marit picked up a large stick and began to beat the headstone. The stick snapped in two. Marit hurled the broken pieces into the woods. She was unarmed now, but Lola felt no easier. She saw Marit place her hands on the stone, lifting and tugging, trying to dislodge it and yank it out of the earth. When the stone would not give, she pounded it with her fists, crying aloud from frustration or the pain in her hands.

Lola started forward. Marit might hurt herself badly. Then a shock of realization forced her back: "The picture. The dead girl in the picture in the wallet." Lola grasped the fence-slats to hold herself steady. When the shock passed she felt cold and numb. Marit was down on her knees digging, doglike, sending earth from the grave flying back between her legs. Digging was tiring; the fit would wind down in time.

In this state of possession, rooting and digging and talking to herself, Marit was like a stranger to Lola—like those women on city buses who wear surgical masks and layers of woolen clothing in the summer. Lola moved to the back of the bus to avoid these women, or got off many blocks before her stop. She kept her distance now from her friend, whose back had been turned for the duration of the seizure, who might have been any casual mad person, inspiring a kind of queasy curiosity. Lola began to move to the edge of the fence, walking slowly, so that she could approach Marit from the side and startle her less. The digging had stopped, but Marit was still on her knees. Lola was nearly abreast of her.

Lola could not have made her heart cold enough to shut out what she saw. Her friend was smearing dirt across her face, rubbing the grave-dirt into her face and hair, taking a handful of dirt at a time and crumbling it between her hands, making it fine and powdery so that it would spread better. She spread it on her face in a circular motion, away from the center, as if she were applying foundation makeup in liquid form. The tears she was crying made the fine dirt wet and smoother to work with. While she smeared on the runny black paste, using only the tips of her fingers, she looked up at the sky, at the tops of the cedars swaying. She shook her head gently, in denial, and patted and smoothed and rubbed, not forgetting her neck or the section under her chin.

Lola went over and crouched down in front of her, sitting on her heels. There had been no need to worry about surprising her. Marit was not disturbed by her presence, or interrupted. She had blackened her face completely, except for her ears. Her changeable eyes had lost any tinge of gray; they were a queer light green in her boyish blackamoor's face.

Lola reached out and took one of Marit's muddy hands.

"What am I going to do with you?" she asked.

Marit met her eyes. She seemed to recognize her, because she held Lola's hand more tightly.

"Is there a baptismal font in the chapel? We could wash you off there. I can't take you down to the lake. You'd scare the children. I'll take you back to my place and put you under the shower. Are you finished here? Have you done what you came to do?"

Marit pulled away and pointed at the headstone. She scooped up more dirt and pressed it into the carving, scooping and pressing with both hands, as if she thought she could erase the name and the inscription.

Lola spoke to herself, not to Marit. "I am not a good friend. I should not have let this happen."

Lola looked at Marit. She was rubbing her eyes with her dirty fists. She was as tired as a child who has been kept up past its bedtime. Lola got up and pulled Marit to her feet. She led her out of the churchyard. Marit followed without protesting and did not look back. Lola helped her into the jeep. She found a traveling pillow and propped it behind Marit's head. She was fast asleep before Lola could start the motor.

SEVEN

By eight o'clock on Friday morning, Marit had been sleeping for fifteen hours—since five o'clock the afternoon before, when Lola had put her down on top of her own bed and covered her with a cotton quilt and a light blanket laid over it. Except for a brief visit to the main house to collect the weekend menus, which had to be typed, and to check the freshness of the flower arrangements in the living room, Lola had been sitting all night in the armchair across from the bed, drowsing at intervals or reading under the light of a standing lamp. She had muffled the lampshade by draping it with a slip and a nightgown, so that it cast a very dim glow and did not wake Marit.

Marit's sleeping behavior did not seem to warrant a night watch. She lay flat on her back and shifted, twice, to each side. She did not pluck at the coverlet or murmur in-

coherencies; she did not toss or frown to indicate the throes
of nightmare. She slept with her mouth open, but Lola knew
that she had always done that—Luba had warned Marit
that no one would marry her if they could see her that
way.

Lola should have been reassured by Marit's regular
breathing, but it was the future that she was keeping watch
over, not this present sleep. Lola loved Marit better than
any sister, and when she looked ahead she saw no happiness
for her.

"Gabriel is saner than you are, Gabriel is a professional
sane person": Marit had tossed this remark off lightly, as if
her interest were in coining a phrase. It had not fallen
lightly on Lola's ears. Marit was like a wild creature, resis-
tant to domestication and confinement. She had no more
place in the coupled world than Lola did. It was the job of a
husband to shear, quell, tame, leash, whittle, and pare
down. Lola could not see Marit as a new draftee, lined
up to enter the married ranks, getting her hair chopped off
with her oddness, handed a suit of clothes which would
blend her in with the others.

Love seemed to have opened up like a pit at Marit's
feet. It took some people that way the first time, but it
portended no better for any times to come. Lola had
watched the impact of love on the girls in her graduating
class; love had carved out their innards, leaving them with a
hole in the middle like a piece of modern sculpture. One day
they were dense and intractable; the next, you could see
right through them. There were rumors around of a love
that enhanced and tonified, that had the strengthening
effects of beef tea or a football training breakfast, but she
had never seen a living example of it.

Lola herself wanted sport and pleasure. Above all, she wanted no emotion that would invade her privacy. But her friend, who had pledged herself to important work, who was scratchy, impatient, and willful, who had all the traits of someone who should never live with anybody, had planted herself in the way of love like a young sapling trying to grow on a bluff swept by high winds. The sapling will bend, and eventually does break; it can never grow to its full height where it is situated.

Lola could not rest imagining Marit's future. Her legs ached and her back ached from sitting in the chair so long. It was seven-forty-five by the clock, and the sunlight had been strong for some time. She raised the blind to let the light wake Marit, and went into the kitchen to fix two breakfast trays. Marit liked breakfasts that reminded her of Paris, so Lola heated milk to pour with the coffee, sliced a flute of French bread baked by Mrs. Gilliam's cook, and put apricot jam and sweet butter into little white pots. She was scooping coffee into the percolator basket when she heard the shuffling of socks on linoleum, and felt two arms twined around her waist. Marit was clinging to her and scratching her nose on her shoulder. A scoop of coffee went half in the basket and half on the counter.

"Can't we eat in here?" said Marit. "Trays in bed make me feel like an invalid."

Lola turned around and inspected Marit closely, lifting her chin and taking a good look at her fingernails.

"Brush your teeth and throw cold water on your face. The coffee will be ready in two shakes."

Marit smiled at her. Lola never showed the wrong kind of sentiment. She never asked how you were, or repeated the question ten seconds later, after you had assured her sincerely that you were fine. Marit told her so.

"Why should I ask?" said Lola, replacing the trays with placemats. "You're as tough as the back end of a shooting gallery."

Marit sat down and dipped a spoon into the jam pot. "I thought I was. Apparently there's a fault in my psyche. The St. Gabriel fault, don't you know."

Lola frowned. This statement sounded like flippancy, or self-parade.

"Since you want to use the analogy, why can't you run for your life when you know the quake is coming?"

"Because I can't. I'm the earthquake and the victim. I also record the shocks."

Lola set down the percolator so hard that coffee splashed out of the spout.

"I do not admire melodrama. Keep that fancy talk for your memoirs. The way you're going, you're not going to live to write them."

"It's not fancy talk, Lolly." Her head was bowed. "It's how it feels."

Lola took her hand and squeezed it. She was frightened of any more tears.

"I have no business to flare up like that. I haven't got the sense God gave a chicken. A friend isn't good for much if she refuses to listen."

"This friend is," said Marit, whose eyes were blurry. "This friend makes café au lait and heats the French bread."

"I did get you cleaned up. I want credit for that. You're very obedient when you're torpid." Lola poured the coffee and handed Marit her cup. "I didn't wash your hair; I just brushed it. I couldn't have you going to sleep with a wet head."

Marit buttered her bread, dipped an end into her coffee, and held it there until it was properly soaked. Little globules of fat floated on top of the liquid.

"I don't like this," Marit said. Lola looked up. "I don't mean my breakfast. I don't like to be in love if it makes me do strange things."

"Some people shouldn't be in love," said Lola. "I'm not sure most women shouldn't."

"If I fall apart, what will happen to my animals? You know what people think. They think that someone like me only cares about animals because we feel as helpless as they are."

"Bears and wolves are not helpless, honey. They can kill a man."

"If it's one to one, they can; but men hunt in gangs. Do you remember that newspaper headline? 'SKIPPER SAVES DOG AS CREW DROWNS'?" Lola shook her head. "I read it to you at the time. You do remember. The captain kept his Labrador in the skiff and let three crewmen hang on to the lifeboat in frigid water. Two of them died. Gabriel wouldn't understand that, but I understand it."

Marit was scraping the sides of the jam pot with her knife. Lola tilted her chair, reached over to the cabinet, and pulled out a new jar of marmalade.

"You talk like Gabriel is your fate, or a curse." She opened the jar. "Look how strong you are. You snapped right back. Look at your appetite. You're making a fine old mess on my table; wipe the crumbs off your face."

"Gabriel is always right and I'm always wrong. I hate being wrong."

"Then end it." Lola flourished her napkin. "Pull out. Cut it off. Say goodbye. Simple solutions never occur to you romantic people."

Marit's face lit up as if she had found the penny in the Twelfth Night cake. A chunk of bread dropped into her coffee, hovered on the surface, and sank to the bottom of the cup.

"I could. I am not a rabbit. I am going to do it."

"Write a letter." Lola gave a wide grin, the leer of experience.

"That's your ploy. Your little flames never know your address. He would come and find me."

"I got caught once," said Lola. "Did I tell you about young Neetsie?"

"Awf. Pfoof." Marit spluttered her coffee. "Is that prep-school for Anita?"

"Her nose was so perfectly snub." Lola was musing. "There she was, two months after I'd killed it, waiting for the same train at the North Adams Station. She fell at my feet and wrapped her arms around my ankles. She had long hair, too. Mary Magdalene. Very poor taste."

Marit was laughing and nodding and coughing. Some of the coffee had gone down her windpipe. The story came back to her now. Lola had stepped daintily out of her shoes and walked to a taxi, leaving Anita weeping into a pair of patent-leather pumps with flat bows.

Solidarity was running high at Lola's kitchen table. Did she need anyone else in the world, with Lola for a cohort? When they could laugh together like this, every hurt that she was feeling faded and scaled down to size. Laughter aired out her brain and blew away must and shadows, so that she could think like a sensible person whose days had purpose.

Sometime this summer the ponds in the heart of the sanctuary, which were choked with algae, must be dragged with a fine-toothed rake, and arrowhead planted around the shoreline to keep the water clear. The hackberries along the south traverse were crowding and dying. With the help of Herb Frechter, she had to mark and ring the trees which could not be saved. Somewhere by the entrance she had seen a cluster of poisonous red-capped amanitas. She must call Joe Miller, at the zoo, to see if the mushrooms had an odor which would stop an animal from eating them. The sanctuary was a school, and there was more to learn than she could master in a lifetime.

"I have to get on with my day," she said to Lola. "The poor dog is still in his pen; it makes him frantic."

"Well, you're not frantic." Lola kissed her goodbye. "That's all I care about. Don't rob any more graves without me, you hear that, missy?"

Marit raised the middle finger of her left hand for an answer, and banged out the door. She ran down the staircase and jumped to the ground from the seventh step. Inside the jeep, she gunned the motor and played a farewell salute on the horn. Her rattly chariot felt as smooth and responsive as a winged horse. Route 37 was the long way home, ending up on the Old Road boundary of her land. It wound through hills, unlike new 22, but she chose it because she liked taking curves. She had her nerve and her power back, and the sun on her face. Work and love were reconcilable in the sunlight. Her mistakes were pardonable.

Her first image of Gabriel appeared to her, with the beak and the eye of an eaglet, proud and short, and as fierce

as she was, but addicted to mildness. Gabriel made himself
perform feats of moral calisthenics in order to hold his nature in check. Her own demons wore nursery faces in the
daylight; nothing had happened when she let them loose, no
depletion that youth and health could not make up for. She
knew that she frightened Gabriel because he sensed their
kinship; he did not condemn her except to keep rein on
himself. If she saw him so clearly, it made no sense to leave
him. From this pinnacle of energy and high spirits, attacks
of jealousy seemed like hazing rites that any pledge to love's
fraternity must endure.

As she drove on she counted off the only man-made
landmarks along the road: the riding stable, the Hoe-Bowl
alleys (boarded up), the brick laundry houses at the
far edge of the Meyerling property, and the cyclone fence,
topped with four tiers of electrified barbed wire, that
enclosed her own land and its wild tenants. Or almost enclosed it. She had one job to do that took precedence over
clearing algae and ringing trees. For several hundred yards
between herself and the Community, in the northeast corner, the only boundary was a natural one: Yoke Pond, the
deepest spring-fed body of water in the county, lying at the
bottom of an ancient wood, which had never been cleared
or cut for lumber since the first white settlements. Wolves
will rarely swim, and the wood ran straight uphill, but
every day that she delayed installing a fence in this section
raised the odds of their discovery.

Beyond the point where her land began, the Old Road
was unimproved. Marit had petitioned to have the bumps
and potholes left as they were to discourage traffic. The
township made no objection to its largest landowner's whim,
since it saved tax dollars. It took two hands on the wheel to

steer around the pits and to avoid the ditch on the fenced-in side, which was widening yearly. Marit kept her eyes fixed just ahead of her. She did not expect to have to deal with a car from the other direction. The trees were so tall, and the shrubs so thick, that the road was crisscrossed with shadows. She turned on the bright headlamps to help her see.

She did not expect to see a man lunge into the road from the sanctuary side, caught in the beam of her lights and stumbling toward cover, carrying a rifle over his head like a soldier fording a stream. For several yards he ran in the open, alongside the road; then he dove for the bushes, using his gun to force his way through. As she pressed her foot down on the gas pedal she still had a bead on him by the rippling and shaking of the underbrush and the cracking of twigs. If she thought she could run him down, she was spared the temptation; by the time the speedometer read thirty-five, the thickets were still. He had veered off through the trees and would be lost in a field of horse corn.

Marit brought the jeep to a halt with its nose pointed into some briars. For a moment she was strung up between horrors; she thought that she had seen a box with knobs and a speaker attached to the man's belt. Were there snipers still in the preserve who could talk by radio? She had a vision of Swan. Swan was dead. She saw him, as clear as prescience; she saw a hole between his eyes, gray fluid draining from the hole, not red like the blood staining his flank, where a second bullet had pierced him. The gunfire had caught him heading downhill. Gravity flung him over and over until he rolled to the level ground in a dried-up gully, thrown on his side, his neck whipped back as if it were broken, his lip pulled up, baring his teeth in a kind of sneer. Pictures of carnage came to her so fast and red, reel after reel of wasted animal bodies, synchronized with the hollow boom of rifle shot, that Marit had no mind left to call on reason, to wage debate between what she might be imagining and what foretelling. Persons who give in to extremes of emotion get no credit for grace under pressure, or for acts of courage or daring committed in a transport. Those honors go to the straight-backed and imperturbable, not to reeds-in-the-wind or extravagants like Marit Deym. No one would commend her now for closing the doors of the jeep and remembering to pocket the key. No one would note the steadiness of her breathing or remark on her rhythmic pace as she crossed the road. There was no one to watch as she reached for a hold on the cyclone fence and thrust the toes of her sneakers into the diamond-shaped holes made by the links, as she climbed sure and cat-like twelve feet up until her waist was even with four electrified rows of barbed wire, which were vertically aligned, not tilted forward as in prison fences. There were no witnesses, so her record for immoderacy would never be balanced by the calculated risk that she was going to take.

She got one leg over the wire, nearly brushing the barbs. For an instant she swayed on the fence, straddling the wire, holding her arms straight out from her shoulders like a tightrope walker trying out the rope. The next moment she was lying on the ground, stunned by a fall that had started as a jump when one toe, rammed too tight between the links, had caught and thrown her backward into a half gainer. How she had twisted out of a dive in that short descent, to save her head and spine, she would not remember. A long time passed before she remembered anything.

She must have knocked her head, because her head was pounding. The second thing that she felt was a pain in one of her ankles; the third, that the left one was hurting, not the right one. Her body came back alive in bits and pieces: a wrist, a thigh, a buttock, and then their opposites. She became aware of two hands and a pair of feet and she flexed them slowly. There was still a no-man's-land between her pelvis and her neck; she opened her eyes, looked down, and reclaimed her torso. She knew that she was breathing by the rise and fall of her chest, or the material covering her chest, her old blue shirt. "I am banged up but good" she thought with her thinking brain. Then she formed her lips to say "Swan": she had powers of speech.

Some time before dark she might get around to moving, or trying to move. The sun was warm and many birds were singing. The grass felt as soft as a pillow, or perhaps it was her body that was cottony and resistless. Thoughts floated up through her mind like bubbles released from a clamshell buried in sand. She had never been able to rest except under enforcement, or to lie down on her bed without a pile of books. If she tried to sleep in the daytime, she would hear her heartbeat drumming. It frightened her. Watching the sand drain out of the top of the egg timer frightened her. Every wristwatch she had owned got wet, overwound, or smashed. She could never be still in an upright position, either; she stalked like a houseless ghost, making work for her hands. Luba would chide her from her throne of cushions: "You have no repose." And now she was lying on the ground, or floating, without complaint, given up to the blue of heaven. The only organ that was not yet functioning was her will.

The kiss of life was administered by a deerfly. He

landed on her nose and bit into the skin. Marit was up like a shot, swearing and hopping in circles. She had slapped the bridge of her nose, not the fly, with the band of her signet ring. The commotion she made was having an effect on the landscape, as if nature were responding in its fashion to her yelps and pains. The mountain laurel was rocking, its pink flowers bobbling; the wind was blowing through a patch of ferns, except that there was no wind. Marit stopped her dancing, rooted by amazement. That bush with the round red berries was whining and barking. That bush had grown a long gray snout and a hairy tail.

She held out her arms and laughed with relief and joy.

"Who is in there?" she called. "Which ones? Did you come to save me?"

For an answer, the larger bushes rustled and shook. There was a flash of red through the laurel, the rusty-red of a fox's coat. Two brown shapes, thin and loopy, streaked out from behind the ferns—the mated minks, who were heading down to the pond. There was the crashing sound of branches trampled by heavier animals, making their way through the shrubbery back to the safe dim woods. One of the animals had seen her lying stunned on the ground, and she knew which one. He had spread the word to the others and they had gathered for a rescue or a vigil. He must have signaled that their work was done, now that she was on her feet again and lively.

Their leader was still at his post, the last to leave. For one instant his head poked out. The gray muzzle, flecked with white hairs, and the one walleye belonged to the oldest wolf, Swan. Marit bowed from the waist, as if he were able to read this act of deference. By the time she had raised her head he was gone, like the others.

St. Francis of Assisi would have bid the beasts into the open. He would have made them lie down and extend their paws for his touch. He would have caused them to be still while he spoke a blessing over them, or enjoined them not to harry the countryside for food. Marit was born with money, like St. Francis; she had no other qualifications for making miracles. Saints love all creatures equally; Marit loved animals better than human beings. It was no miracle that the animals had rallied around to help her; it was a tendency in their nature, and it spoke of their worth, not hers. Animals were innocent. They were not bad when they lunged and bit in pain or fear, or good when they fetched a slipper or came to heel. Those were human standards, devised for training children.

Nikolai had been raised by children's rules for his protection, since he must live in the world with people. Nikolai would be battering the sides of his pen. It was noon, by the sun overhead, and he had missed two feedings. Marit had half an hour's jog through the sanctuary before she could free him. She would ask Lola to drive her back to the road to retrieve the jeep.

Between three and five on weekend afternoons, teachers and counselors at Meyerling entertained guests of the other sex in their own rooms, which were furnished like little suites, with a sofa and armchairs. Daisy Fellowes had a miniature icebox; Rennie Gaines, the spiritual director, had a tufted kneeler; and Gabriel had a pair of badly foxed bird prints; but the most important fixture of any teacher's room was the doorstop supplied by the Community, a brick covered in various calicoes by a previous cook. The brick doorstops had their own code life: the open position meant that the occupant was holding office hours; halfway open, that he was having a private talk; three-quarters shut, that he was working; fully closed, that he was dressing, undressing, or sleeping. This unwritten code was for the discipline of the teachers, since the blind children treated halfway and three-quarters as fully open. So did the Head Teacher, Henry Dufton, most of the time, although he could only claim to be legally blind. "We are a family," Mr. Dufton liked to say; "we must not keep little secrets from each other."

News of a visitor spread within minutes of his or her arrival. Gabriel lived in the last room but one at the end of a corridor. The room at the far end was a locked linen closet, and the only room across the hall from his was unoccupied during the summer. So far, Marit had counted five faculty people passing by and glancing in, undisturbed by the fact that they had no excuse except inquisitiveness for being in that part of the hall. After the third passerby, she had taken off her sneakers and arranged her chair so that all they would see through the half-open door were her naked feet, calves, and knees. There was no point in letting them go away unrewarded.

When Marit had reached her house at midday, she had found Gabriel sitting on the back steps. If hats had been the fashion, he would have been waiting for her hat in hand. He had enough sense not to speak to her immediately, since she was red in the face from running, and breathing hard. He followed her into the kitchen, where she cut up round steak for Nikolai, and followed her outside again while she opened the malamute's pen. Nikolai jumped up to lick Marit's face, fell on his food dish, wheeled back to nudge his mistress, remembered his dish of raw meat—Gabriel stood by until this frenzy of welcome had died down. Then he asked her very shyly, like a village swain, if she would come to have tea in his room that afternoon. He was on back-up duty all weekend, and he had something important to say to her. Fresh from a miracle, Marit watched him without interest. He hesitated when he spoke. His hands were clasped behind his back. In some scenarios he would have produced a little pasteboard ring box. Only after he had left, or, in fact, had bowed his way out, did she remember that she had considered sending him away.

Two mugs were sitting on the coffee table in Gabriel's room. Marit had finished her tea, but Gabriel's mug was full, and she was alone. The crafts counselor had slipped on wet clay and broken her wrist, and Gabriel was even now letting her substitute into the blind maze, a series of rooms in the basement that were fitted out like a small apartment. All he had to do was to tie a black scarf over the new woman's eyes and instruct her that she would be left there for two hours, with the lights out, during which time she was to take a bath, change into garments that were hanging in one of the closets, find the icebox, and make herself a sandwich, half of which she must leave as evidence of her effort. There was a radio in one of the rooms, but almost none of the initiates ever found it.

Gabriel peered around the door before coming in, as if he expected Marit to be spitting tacks or to be vanished.

"That was a long one," she said, with a pleasant smile.

"She balked," said Gabriel. "I think she's going to cheat."

"How can you tell when they haven't cheated?" asked Marit, trying to keep a good interviewer's distance from her subject.

Gabriel glanced out into the hallway before he answered. He lowered his voice. "Blobs of mayonnaise on the floor."

Then he met her eyes and laughed at himself for whispering. Marit reached for his hand and steered him into the chair across from her. For the moment she had the advantage, and she enjoyed it. Perhaps they could build a friendship out of the romantic rubble.

"There is enough pietistic nonsense floating around here to start a church." She was kind enough to keep her voice from carrying.

"Hold on," said Gabriel. "How can you be effective with blind people if you have no insight into being blind?"

"Oh, wonderful. Admirable. There are monks who sleep in coffins so that they can get insight into being dead."

"Dufton may be a turkey, but he's a genius with children." Gabriel bit his lip, a sure sign that his temper was rising.

"Then everyone who works here should be blind. The maze is a halfway measure. Put out their eyes instead."

Gabriel grew mild. He had decided to practice nonviolence. "Is there some reason why the subject of blindness makes you uncomfortable?"

A flicker of hostility loosened Marit's tongue. "What are they, in the first place? A bunch of overprivileged kids: they could be blind or green."

"I agree," answered Gabriel. "Blindness is a privilege."

Neither one of them heard Daisy Fellowes coming, although she walked with an echo, like a storm trooper. Miss Fellowes never knocked and never apologized. The only grammatical mood that she used was the imperative.

"You have a guest, Gabriel," she announced. She also

talked with an echo. "Miss Deym will have to excuse us. There is a fight in the five tent."

"John?" asked Gabriel, but she had already marched away.

Marit opened her mouth to protest, but she cut herself short. Gabriel raised his palms and shrugged, a gesture of resignation that he had picked up in Cuba. He was hovering at the doorsill, pulled toward her and pulled away from her, pleading without a word. She took him by the shoulders, pointed him down the hall, and gave him a little shove to get him started.

Marit stretched out on the couch with her fingers linked behind her head, smiling at her endless flexibility. She did not feel for a second—or perhaps for a second, but the feeling did not hold—that Gabriel's calls to duty were an act of desertion or disrespect. Up, down, up, down: how busy he was, like a jack-in-the-box coiled to jump when the lid was opened. The jack springs up, head waggling, smiling his painted-on smile, but Gabriel had looked bothered and rebellious, and gone forth to his tasks glancing backward. He wore the institutional life like a hair shirt; at the moment it seemed that the shirt was drawing blood. Just before he went padding after Daisy Fellowes, Marit had seen a wild look in his eyes, as if his eyes had come loose and were rolling in their sockets. Captured birds had that look as well, and hawks who are given over to a novice handler.

Marit thought that the blind children would have that look if their eyes were not dead. This model blind farm, with its euphemistic name, was a cageless zoo where natural instincts were slowly being blunted. Nine- and ten-year-olds slept in the five tent during summer camp season; in three years' time no more fights would break out, wherever they were housed. Meyerling modulated the voices of its wards along with their personalities. A soft, low voice is considered an excellent thing in the blind. By the time they lined up at graduation, dressed in white regardless of their sex, these same scrappy boys and girls would resemble postulants to a contemplative order, with their bowed heads and bowed shoulders, unlined faces, and pallid complexions. Enclosure and meditation are better than any cream or cosmetic for the life of the skin, but not for the condition of the spirit, walled up before its time. If the journey from birth to death spans seven ages, Meyerling wanted its charges to leap from the dependency of childhood to the resignation of old age, skipping the glory or the conflict in between. Meyerling filed the teeth of its young inmates and declawed them, as some heinous owners do with feline pets.

Marit sat up to halt the course of her thoughts. She was faced with indicting Gabriel along with Meyerling. He worked here; therefore he must have bought the message. He had said that blindness was a privilege. Things were looking bad for Gabriel and worse for her illusions. Gazing clear-eyed at the loved one is just as dangerous as looking straight at the Medusa. All these meek and thwarted children, offered up as testimony to the high intentions of their preceptors: Marit's back was to the wall, staving off a vision of Gabriel drawing uplift and humility from the blind for the sake of his conscience, not for their salvation, the sin that all philanthropists are heir to.

Marit stood up and started to pace the room. The room was small and crowded. She did not pace so much as pick her way through the furniture. What girl infected by Romance wants the itch to subside and the swelling to go down? Objectivity was the salve, but she refused it. She was too new to the fevers, knots, breathlessness, waiting, throes, and skipped heartbeats. The machine of Romance had been idling; she cranked it up and opened the throttle wide. Gabriel was like a peregrine, leashed at the leg and hooded, in training for immolation, not for combat. She loved the bird, but not the equipment of self-denial. She had the power to make some inroads on his higher nature. The way to his sense of humor was through his appetites.

The door, exactly half open, swayed to three-quarters. The girl in the doorway advanced with her arms outstretched, holding her palms up to feel for obstacles, like the newly blind. She moved in short, quick steps, then braked. Her hands made contact with the top of an armchair. Marit held her breath and stood as still as an Indian. Two chairs stood between her and the intruder; their inert mass might block the magnetic circuit.

"Gabriel?" said the girl.

Gabriel was the only teacher who was ever called by his first name. The girl turned her face in Marit's direction. Marit recognized her and remembered her live slanted eyes.

"Who are you?" demanded the girl.

Marit did not like to be challenged. All her fine thoughts flew out the window. This was one blind person who did not know her place, this girl with the fancy name, Aimée, who was as plain as an oatcake, actually, who had the sexual assurance of a beauty, who would snake your beau as soon as look at him.

"I can't help you," said Marit. "He is somewhere on the grounds with Miss Fellowes."

"I have to see him," ordered Aimée. "I had another one of my nightmares."

"At five o'clock in the afternoon?" Marit did not know when to quit.

"He knows what to do. He has healing hands. Please tell him I want him."

"What is your name?"

"Aimée Dupuis." The girl frowned in some surprise, like a movie star who is asked by a bank clerk to prove her signature.

Marit watched her retreat. She did not like what the girl had said. Ministers and doctors lay on hands, on the patient's head or on the affected part directly. What part of a troubled sleeper has a nightmare? If the seat of the unconscious is the brain, the brain is safely lodged above the neck. But dreams are the fumes of the sexual furnace, which is located in the belly and below. Where were Gabriel's blunt healing workman's hands getting to? "Another nightmare" implied that he had held more than one healing session. Did he work through the clothes or on bare skin? The body of this blind healee was rounded beyond her years. As she had felt her way out of the room, Marit had observed a perfect muscular crupper, like a well-made pony's. Any man—philanthropist, poet, or healer—would enjoy the feel of that backside under his fingers. Marit became aware of a slow, pulling sensation in her lower torso. It is one of jealousy's dirty secrets that it causes an engorgement of blood.

The harried suitor was back, reaching out to her, hoping to make some compensation for his absence. If a sweet disarray is exciting in women's clothes, Gabriel had achieved the counterpart for men—the shirt unbuttoned to the third button, the cuffs folded back and rolled unevenly above the elbows, judicious grass stains on his rumpled linen trousers. Marit tried to summon her recent detachment; it was no match for arousal. She let him pull her into his arms and hold her against him. Her own arms hung down at her sides. This ambiguous jealous lust had turned her to stone.

"You had a caller," she said. She was able to meet his eyes.

He butted the chair with his fist. "Who wants a piece of me now?"

Marit grinned as if she sympathized sincerely. "A girl with one of those little-princess names. A French name."

Gabriel became alert and professional. "Aimée. The new senior. A case of hysterical blindness."

"She did mention a nightmare." Marit wondered if the hysterical factor would reduce the girl's pathos and allure, or serve to increase it.

"That's not good. I'll have to take care of it." Gabriel addressed her as one colleague to another. There was no wild, torn look in his eyes. He had changed from a falcon into the falconer.

"How will you take care of it?" asked Marit.

"I never know from one to the next. It depends on the subject matter of the dream."

"Does she dream in color?" Marit's throat was closing as if strong fingers had a grip on it. Gabriel was talking about his work. That was a sign, or even the cornerstone, of intimacy. The thought did not soothe her.

"Would that matter? She is always a victim. Wild dogs licking her face, nuns holding scissors, parrots wheeling over her bed."

"Sexual uproar." To her own ears, Marit's voice sounded like a mouse squeak.

Gabriel had heard her. He did not seem to like the notion. "She is still a child, Marit."

Marit felt the reproof. She would have taken a pair of scissors to him herself if they had been handy. The little princess was inventing dreams in order to bind him to her. She was another Francesca, one of those girls who had been a special case from babyhood, another idol in Gabriel's female martyrology, another one of his opportunities for self-transcendence, unlike scaly, earthbound Marit, that sulphurous toad, who would drag him away from the light and feast on his blood.

Gabriel was thumbing through a row of books on an upper shelf. He pushed aside several and pulled out one that had fallen behind. It was a narrow book with a glossy cream-colored jacket. She could read the black print on the cover before he took it: *Selected Poems of Rainer Maria Rilke*. Gabriel was pioneering in bibliotherapy.

"I can't wait for you," said Marit.

He turned around and gave her a look of infinite sweetness.

"I wish you could," he said, and left the room.

If Gabriel heard the sound of his traveling alarm clock smashing against the wall, he did not stop in his tracks, forsake his mission, and fly back to investigate. He was too far down the hall to hear his desk chair kicked to the floor.

EIGHT

BISHOP MEYERLING had fallen in love, once in his life and stunningly, before he was a bishop or even a dean, and before he was misshapen in the First World War. It was a great love, in the style of the period, with an odor of violets and chivalry, unrequited because his lady was married and of severe virtue. Lucy Backhouse was a heroine of the period, with piles of soft hair pinned up high, dark untrimmed eyebrows ("thy brows like brushing wings"), and smoky patches under her eyes—a sign, it seemed to him, that this angel would not dwell long among mortal men.

Colman Meyerling cherished this society portraitist's image of his beloved, but the angel was made of tougher fiber. Jack Backhouse, who had cornered the market in coffee, was a permissive husband, and not a vain one. He had not married Lucy for her beauty, but for her coffee shares. His commodities empire was the only ornament to his manhood that he needed. Jack's respect for hard work and his lack of interest in his wife were on Lucy's side. When she spent her days at a charity hospital, and refused to attend all but the six or seven balls, benefits, and opening nights that couples in the Backhouses' position could not decently evade, she was not violating their marital covenant. She was giving Jack more time at his office on Battery Park.

Without Jack's protection Lucy would have been a scandal. If she had taken up hospital work before she had married him, she would have remained a spinster, an untouchable like the poor and the cancerous and the syphilitic whom she cared for. Lucy with the queenly walk and noble brow did not wheel book carts through wards of convalescents, soothing their irritability with a smile, plumping up a pillow, deflecting harsh sunlight by angling a shutter. Her patients were emergencies and incurables. She put her hands on them. She saw parts of the body that should always be covered by clothing. She heard ugly words spoken to her because she had swabbed too deep, or ripped away a dressing. At the end of a morning her apron was splashed with blood and pus.

Lucy had studied nursing by apprenticeship, not in school. She would not have been allowed to go to school even if she had chosen a sanitary subject like the classics. Her tutor had been dismissed when she was seventeen, the year before her coming-out. When she was twenty-one and a married woman with access to her own money, she had gone to see a cousin of her mother's, a surgeon on the board of Bathgate Charity, and offered him a bribe large enough to pay the salaries of three new staff members. What she asked in return was the chance to learn by working. Her first job was as a mangler in the Bathgate laundry.

Colman Meyerling heard of her work before he was shipped to France. He arranged to have himself seated next to her at one of the rare formal dinners she attended. If his orders had not come through, he would never have been so forward. After the required ten minutes with his partner on the other side, he turned to Lucy and praised her for her life of sacrifice. He got the tartest, most dismissive answer.

Lucy was not a saint. Sickness and misery brought out her Dutch inheritance. She approached a patient like a compulsive housekeeper tackling a room. Sores, abscesses, infections, and twisted limbs were disorderly and inefficient. A cured and tidy body brought her peace of mind, short-lived, however, since the amount of disease and suffering in the world was at least equal to the grains of soot that piled up on clean windowsills every day. What Lucy had said to the future bishop—the exact words changed in his memory with time—was "The only place, sir, for martyrdom is on the battlefield." It took all his restraint to keep from boasting that he had enlisted.

Colman dreamed of her throughout the war, when he was not having more tainted thoughts about women closer to hand. While his back was mending, he imagined that she had chosen war work, that she would appear in a halo of light and make him straight again. These daydreams might have brought on melancholia if the nurse on his ward had not been pleased to dispel his tensions. When he came home newly humpbacked, with plans for entering the clergy, he did not try to see her. He put Lucy away, along with his polo sticks, riding crop, and silver punch bowls.

Fifteen years later, the Bishop built a dwarf Gothic chapel on his grounds at Meyerling, and dedicated it to St. Lucy, virgin and martyr. Not long after the chapel was finished, he received word that John Backhouse had died on a trip to the Amazon. It is clear that the Bishop pondered bringing suit to the widow, but custom required that she spend twelve months in mourning and seclusion. At the end of the year (1934), Lucy married the chief of staff at Bathgate Charity, who was a specialist in diseases of the joints.

The Bishop indulged himself in a useless show of spite. As soon as he learned the news of Lucy's marriage, he marched into the chapel, ripped the altar cloth athwart, and stamped it underfoot. Then his eye fell on the statue of St. Lucy, standing in a little niche behind the pulpit. He stood on a pile of hymnals, seized the doll-sized wooden image by the neck, and hurled her the length of the chapel, where she broke on the wall. The pile of hymnals slid to the floor, and the Bishop with them. The heavy cast that was put on his hip served to punish him for many months for his blasphemous act.

Now English ivy covered the gaudy little building. Ivy also darkened the stained-glass window, which showed Lucy's eyes being snatched out by Roman soldiers and used to play marbles; and had been called by reviewers in architectural journals "the goriest window in the non-Spanish-speaking world." The chapel had been gutted and stripped of the altar block and pews. Folding chairs were stacked in piles inside the vestibule. The building was now used for assemblies, chorus rehearsals, morning meditations, and classes like Gabriel's poetry workshop that needed exercise room. Marit loved the chapel and thought that God probably still kept it on His checklist. She loved the story of the

Bishop's undeclared passion and his revenge—Luba's version of the story, therefore highly colored.

A double row of Scotch pines backed the apse end of the chapel. Their needles screened the narrow windows, which were set with clear glass—old, hand-poured panes that were bubbly and distorting. Marit pushed through the outer branches and made a space to peer through. She did not need the antique glass to queer her vision. Gabriel's workshop was held on Mondays after supper. It was seven o'clock, and the class was half over. She had had no sign from Gabriel since the girl with the nightmare had claimed him. The girl was there in the circle of students seated on the floor, directly across from Gabriel in the circle, leaning back on her elbows with her knees raised, wearing little shorts.

Marit had rarely spied before, except by accident. Once in New York, during a long school break at Easter, she had left a subscription dance early without her escort. With the back-door key, borrowed from the doorman, she had let herself into the apartment very cautiously. Her plan was to hide in the laundry room until an hour that was late enough to convince her mother she had had a good time, and then go downstairs and ride up again by the front elevator. She had removed her shoes and started down the servants' hallway when she heard Luba's voice from the kitchen: "I will not stand this." Marit sighed, turned around, and got ready for a scolding. Luba spoke again, so low that she was almost whispering: "You ask me to escape a sick man." There was a short pause, the sound of choked tears, and the receiver banging down on the hook. Marit was too relieved to consider what she had heard.

That was one count of eavesdropping acquitted, which

left a charge of prying to examine. After school one day, she had been sorting through her father's old shirts; he never gave, or threw, anything away. Oversized men's shirts were the fashion, and Vlado's were made of silk. At the bottom of a drawer her hand had fastened on a wad of paper. She found twelve suicide notes in all, the same note with small changes in wording, like a literary exercise. Vlado was perfectly well at the time; she had just left him in the pantry, taking the electric can opener apart. There was a third charge of snooping pending, but Marit no longer felt that she had to answer for searching Gabriel's wallet. She saw no need to be fair, since love was a war of nerves.

There was science to Marit's spying on Gabriel's workshop, and it was based on deductive reasoning: she had come to prove a hypothesis, not to form one. Jealous people are logical beings. Their logic is inflexible and airtight. Marit approached her subject with the loftiest disinterest. All her findings would go against her; yet she was never tempted to juggle data in her favor.

Gabriel was a helper. She offered him nothing to prick his sense of responsibility as this young girl did. Marit was not blind, dead, maimed, halt, leprous, indigent, or meek. Sexual passion would never hold him; it was too rich a diet. In the long run he was vegetarian in matters of sex. He would never give her a rival who was her own size, only a trail of beggars with their hands out, stinking of weakness. Over the last forty-eight hours he had made her snivel, like one of them. She could win him back if she told him how she had waited for him, staying close to the house like a tethered dog, retching on a mouthful of soup, flicking her thumbnail inside the nail of her ring finger at the rate of the second hand circling the face of the clock.

Marit had not changed her clothes since Saturday afternoon, groomed her hair, or washed her teeth, except to rinse out her mouth occasionally with cold water. The boggy smell of her shirt and trousers was not her own. Nikolai had gone swimming and come home with his coat wet and mud-caked, needing affection. Marit was pleased with her unkempt body. The lines of dirt around her wrists, the frayed ends of her shoelaces gave her integrity in her rejected state. The girl with the French name, spreading her knees in Gabriel's direction, was as fresh and washed as a child brought in by the nurse to kiss its parents good night. Those same knees had a rosy tinge that matched her cheeks. She would have a closed child's slit between her legs, the kind that men preferred, covered with fine blonde down.

The lower windowpane, attached by a chain, was hanging open. The bottom panes of all the windows could be let down to supply ventilation, although the chapel was built of granite, which locked in the cool. Marit heard the sound of Gabriel's voice and pushed in a little closer to make out the words. She could anticipate what he was saying. If outside noises drowned out parts of his talk, she could supply the missing words herself.

Gabriel moved around the circle of students as he spoke, using his hands to express a point. Most sighted people were sensory morons, he was explaining, smug and happy with the visible surfaces of things, connecting nothing seen with the unseen, letting their eyeballs do their living for them. Eyesight kept experience at a safe remove; eyesight led to labeling, judging, and other restrictive mental habits. Sighted people were brains without bodies who called the other senses the animal faculties. Gabriel looked up at the vaulted ceiling like an actor giving a soliloquy.

Whose standard ranked psychic gifts as " 'second' sight"?
Of what use were eyes for telepathy, or precognition, or
discourse with God? Blind Homer, blind Milton, St. Teresa
in bliss—there were more names in Gabriel's roster of the
transcendent sightless; but pine needles were brushing
Marit's nostrils, and she sneezed.

She sneezed loud enough to have to duck down for
cover. She waited for sounds of alarm or the rush of
stampeding children. Then she heard the thin notes of a
melody with a heavy beat, music from a ballet that was too
familiar to recall. She raised herself up by inches and looked
inside. Gabriel was clapping his hands, exciting his pupils to
their feet to begin the movement portion of the workshop.

Three times over, surefooted and rapt, nine youngsters
swayed through a repetition of the vowels, leaving off *y*.
The ballet music came from a tape recorder, music bland
enough not to dictate individual moves, nor to overpower
the chanting of vowel sounds and words incarnating vowels.
She heard Gabriel's voice over the music, leading the exercise: vowels were like gems in a matrix of iron ore; vowels
were the life and soul of a word; consonants were the hide
and bone.

There was a series of little mutinies inside the group.
Some of the children had begun to act out words of their
own.

"Ah, ah!" One boy jumped to the *a*, his skinny chest
swollen with the indrawn breath.

"O, *o*, hole," moaned Aimée, tracing a circle and slump-
ing over into it.

"Sting!" yelled a fat boy next to her, making conductor's
passes at an imaginary orchestra with his hands.

Gabriel knew when to get his charges back in line. He

called each one to his place and pointed all of them toward the center of the circle. There were two or three whom he had to sit down bodily. When they were gathered into a circle on the floor, he asked them what they had discovered during the exercise.

The fat boy took over. "*I* is a nervous itchy vowel!"

It was a signal for riot. Suddenly nine fidgety blind adolescents all wanted to do *i*, began impersonating the whole phonetic spectrum from *ih* to *eee*, hopping and shrieking, until Gabriel cupped his hands around his mouth to magnify his voice, ordering them back to the use of *i* in poetry, and got them droning and stressing the couplet to Shakespeare's Sonnet XXVII:

> Lo, thus, by day my límbs/by níght my mínd,
> For thee and for myself/no quiet fínd.

The chapel emptied out as if a drain had been unstopped. The boys whooped through the door, celebrating their freedom. The girls clustered at the entrance and moved out as one, like a single-celled organism. Marit stayed behind the pines, watching Gabriel unplug the tape recorder and roll an upright piano back against the wall. She was losing hold of her purpose. A teacher is an impersonal figure, and Gabriel took on stature in front of a class. He had told her that after teaching he felt flushed with stimulation, that his body felt light, that he would run up three flights of stairs on the way to his room. It would do her no good to intrude on his exaltation. If she appeared in his path, she would break his stride, like a stone or a root over which a runner stumbles. The act of spying had drawn some of the evil out of her. She

had better slink back to the road where she had left her
car.

Gabriel walked over to a metal plate on the wall. The
first two switches he pressed darkened the apse and the
vestibule. The third switch controlled every light except
four spots in the ceiling. Into that spotlit central space
Aimée made an entrance, holding her head up and taking
her time, with confidence in her movements. There is always one student who hangs around after class, asking for
extra reading, or pretending to be confused about a point in
the lecture. Marit had seen these girls making up to the
teacher, hugging their textbooks and ducking their chins as
if they had conquered years of shyness in order to voice one
question. This girl in shorts, with honey-colored skin,
seemed to have arrived by preappointment, so that Gabriel's
attention was her due. She occupied the lighted nave with
the ease of a born performer.

Gabriel did not keep her waiting. He dropped his book
bag and hurried up to her, reaching out a hand to stroke her
hair. They kept a short space between them, the distance
reserved for private conversations, that electric interval
which is only inches wider than a lovers' tryst. Marit heard
the murmur of their voices, but the words they were saying
did not carry. She could see smiling and nodding and other
signs of animation, the give and take of two people who are
already in perfect agreement. Gabriel and Aimée were
physically matched. They were equal in height. She was
curved; he was flat. He was brown; she was gold. Marit and
Gabriel, under that light, would be ill-assorted, hard and
lean like two boys. No feature of their two silhouettes would
show the pull between male and female. They did not make
a couple.

Marit had learned to stand with her arms crossed over her breasts to disguise their size. This upstart blind girl used her breasts to express herself, the way Latins use their hands. Gabriel's hands were jammed into the pockets of his trousers. Was he forcing himself to contain them, since of their own accord they would cup, knead, mold, unbutton, and stroke? There had been male teachers at Marit's female college; half the faculty were men. Any candidate for Master of Arts was fair game and no danger to their jobs; by unwritten rule they did not poach on undergraduates. There had to be a law at Meyerling, not unwritten but codified, preventing Gabriel from moving one step closer to this girl of sixteen, a minor and a cripple.

As if Marit had willed it with that part of her mind that could still act in his interest, Gabriel took a step backward. His hands came out of his pockets, and for one instant it seemed as if the assignation had ended. Then he moved forward, grasped the girl's shoulders, and placed a kiss like a star at the center of her forehead, holding his lips to her forehead long enough to brand her. Her chin sunk to her chest. She stood limp between his hands. He turned her around and guided her a few steps in the direction of the chapel door. He left her abruptly and walked into the shadowy aisle, stiffening his neck in order not to look back at her.

Marit had begun to see everything with captions, as if she were perusing a series of eighteenth-century erotic prints. This last scene was entitled "The False Renunciation," in which the shepherd forswears the lady for the sake of her honor and the distance between their stations. The next picture would be "The Happenstance Reunion," and show the lady weeping in the glade that had sheltered their meetings, while the shepherd approaches, with eyes cast down, on the same sad pilgrimage. "The Ecstasy" is the last number in the series, a flurry of petticoats and a rubble of crooks and slippers. The jealous person, like the contemplative, reaches a high degree of single-pointed focus. Marit had fixed her mind on one interpretation, ruling out commonplace human motives which had the power to comfort her. The teacher might have been persuading his blind pupil to take the walk back to the main house without assistance. The pupil, a nubile girl, might have been making female overtures to the teacher, who had checked them with fatherly treatment. The pupil might have wanted the teacher's time to discuss a problem, and been put off, since he was expected at other activities.

The lights in the chapel went out. Marit could not hear Gabriel's footsteps across the floor, but she heard the door close. She crawled out from behind the pine trees, hurting her knee on a half-buried rock, and made her way around the side of the chapel, silent and hunched down. There was a path that led straight to the mansion, lined on both sides with yews. Gabriel was on the path, walking briskly, his book bag slung over one shoulder.

Marit darted across to the farther side, where the yews were tall enough to hide her if she bowed her neck. There was a cover of needles on the ground which would deaden her footfall. As she moved, leaning sideways, she peered through openings in the evergreens. She was all eyes, she was one huge eye, floating like the moon—which was rising —among the branches.

It was clear to her that the girl would not take dismissal easily. She would dawdle up ahead, pacing herself, laying another trap for Gabriel, who would have used up his resistance dodging the first one. Marit wanted proof to end the cycle of suspicion, not thinking that she would then need firmer evidence and harder clues, that she would have to pile up certainty after certainty, the way incurables try new doctors and stronger remedies. She had witnessed a kiss on the forehead, which portended a kiss on the mouth. When she caught them embracing mouth-to-mouth, she could infer the act of rapture. If she saw them naked and joined, her knowledge would still be partial. They might have glutted their appetite in one bout, or whetted it for future engagements. How many return engagements and on what terms? Would they be using each other's bodies or making love? The more Marit knew, the more her knowledge would fail her.

The path ended at a line of rhododendrons bordering the expanse of lawn that surrounded the manor house. The windows of Meyerling cast bands of light over the lawn. Gabriel's figure receded slowly from her view, until he became a black shape climbing the terrace steps. She could not see him crossing the terrace; then his outline appeared in the open door. Marit waited for the girl to make her move. The lawn was empty. The door to the terrace closed. The girl must have gone inside by another entrance.

Marit felt like a plainclothesman on a stakeout after a twelve-hour watch with nothing to report. The material of her trousers was sticking to one knee. She pulled at the cloth and winced in pain. Her banged knee had bled and now she had opened the sore. The Berkshire Hills can cool off fast when the sun goes down. Marit's arms were bare. She was wearing an old shirt with the sleeves ripped out at the armholes. There was a piece of chocolate wrapped in tinfoil in

one of her pockets. It had melted a little and conformed to
the curve of her hip. She ate the chocolate and found that
she was no less hungry. Her plans were blocked, just as her
endurance was dwindling. Her imagination goaded her on,
but lazily, as if she were writing a story: penetrate Meyerling through boiler room; sneak up three flights; take up
station in vacant room opposite Gabriel's; observe girl gain-
ing admittance . . . Her mind lost the thread. Her body
wanted some respite. A picture of the living room at home
glowed in her memory, like a place she could not get back
to: the same house that she was never at ease in after dark,
the same living room with its massive furniture and velvet
draperies, scaled down, in her recollection, to cottage size,
with a fire burning in the grate, for cheer as much as for
warmth.

Hot milk, flannel robes, Fig Newtons, wood smoke;
tuned pianos, wildlife journals, snoring malamutes. Building
this roster of small pleasures as a charm against sadness and
the chilly air, Marit began to walk to keep her limbs in
motion, paying little attention to the course her steps were
taking. She might have wandered any distance in distraction
if a noise, somewhere on her left, had not aroused her.
A bleating or a cheeping noise, on a faltering note, without
the mechanical tone produced by birds or sheep. Then
a ragged sound, like breath catching in the throat. Someone
needed help. There was a full infirmary at Meyerling and
a nurse in residence. Marit listened again. The same rough,
choking sound. It did not weep. It could not be a person.
She forced herself to keep still. Even injured, a frightened
animal would try to run. It would see her as an enemy,
not a rescuer. She widened her eyes to look for signs of
movement.

Marit had good night vision. She did not have to use it. The moon, which was almost full or almost waning, was high enough now to shine through the tallest trees. For the first time since she had strayed off the chapel path, Marit took stock of the space around her. She glanced backward to get her bearings by the lights of Meyerling. She wheeled to one side, then the other. The house was missing. Her gaze traveled upward, following a cloudy shaft of moonlight, measuring the long and branchless trunks of giant trees whose crowns seemed to brush the surface of the moon. Her eyes had adjusted to the mist that hung over the forest floor. There was no scrub in this wood, only scattered bushes and a few creepers putting out tendrils over a mat of fallen leaves. The bark of the trees stood out in high relief, scaly and deeply furrowed. The trunks of these trees had grown to their full diameter, three or four feet across, the sign of victory in a fight for space that had lasted centuries.

This was the ancient hardwood forest—black maple, oak, and hemlock—that had survived uncut between her land and Meyerling. It belonged to neither property. Her parents and the Bishop had willed it to the State of Massachusetts, with the condition that it be preserved intact and used for study, not for recreation. After her parents had died, Marit had come a short way into the woods with the state surveyor, by daylight, in late November when the leaves were down. So much sky showed through the bare branches at that season that the trees had seemed diminished. By night, under spreading canopies of leaves, they regained the magnitude that fit their age.

An old wood does not reach its full size by welcoming man and his devices, his axes, sugar taps, and specimen bags. Marit could feel the trees close ranks, like a nation-state preparing for invasion. There are huge stones in England, in Cornwall, like the megaliths at Stonehenge; and there are tales about those stones, that men have gone too near them at certain phases of the moon and been found dead near their base with their bones broken, as if the stones had embraced and crushed the life from them. These trees were younger than the Cornish stones, and might not have attained the strength to kill, but Marit knew, with every hair and every pore, that they were merging forces to expel her and whatever living being lay whining near enough to hear but out of eyeshot.

She had no choice if she was going to help the creature but to move toward it and flush it out of hiding. She walked cautiously, trying not to graze the tree trunks, but her footsteps thrashed through the crumbled leaves, the louder for the mist which broadcast sound. There was a thrashing, in answer to her progress, ten yards away, at the edge of a little clearing. The animal that started up from cover, forced by panic into the open, cowering in the open in the hunched position in which it had been hiding, had two legs, like Marit, and the marks of the female sex.

Marit dropped down on all fours, as if she were the one in danger, not the rescuer, and her safety depended on keeping out of sight. There was no danger to Marit from the figure in the clearing. The figure could not see her. She could not see the moon overhead or the plumes of mist or the rutted tree trunks. She did not seem able to talk, in any normal human language. Her mouth opened and closed, murmuring confused syllables, repeating a pattern of high-pitched sounds that had no meaning, like a penitent saying the rosary.

What kind of penance would Gabriel set himself when

he found out that he had let his protégée lose her way? A good teacher does not make cripples of his students, so he had pushed her off to walk the ground unaided. He would make himself pay for his miscalculation. He would redouble his guard, valuing the lost lamb more than all his self-reliant charges, who could dress and feed themselves, tell north from south, saddle horses, and beat him at chess. This was a shorn lamb huddled in the clearing, shuffling in slow circles, fleeced of her wiles and assets, her breasts drooping and her fine legs tracked with scratches.

On all fours, in the hunting posture common to beasts, Marit started forward, poised and eager, like a ferret out for rabbits. She felt herself grow hunched and prognathous, dim and feral as the ape-man. Her hands seemed immense and hamlike. Her fingers brushed the ground as she moved. Blood pounded in her temples and facial arteries. Her eyes were slits.

A ferret glides; a cobra slithers. Larger hunters make clumsy errors in their footwork, tipping the odds in favor of their prey. Marit's knee pressed down on a branch half-covered by leaves. The branch cracked and broke. The blind girl started to run. A thud and a moan. She had run into a tree. She was down and scrambling back onto her feet, and felled again as she lurched into a second trunk. This time she stayed down and crawled, dragging herself forward on her arm, keeping the other raised to fend off nearing trees. When one arm tired, she lifted the other, sweeping it back and forth in front of her, striking the back of her hand, more painful than the palm, against a tree trunk, flailing the bruised hand, her body sagging lower and lower, expended, until finally she was moving on her elbows.

Marit was erect now, hunting on two feet as humans

do, working her prey by deliberate moves. They had come to a darker region of the forest, where the denser growth of trees blocked out the light. Marit felt her smooth-skinned quarry more than saw her, guided as surely in her direction as a water witch is led by the forked branch slanting downward. Her hearing had grown sharp and stoatlike; she could see with the backs of her arms and the soles of her feet, even through her shoes. Her feet picked out soft patches, lichens and woodruff, to damp her tread when she wanted to give the girl a rest. When she wanted to scare her onward, she found loose stones to roll, puffballs to burst, dry twigs to snap. There was no hurry. She had the blind girl on a long leash. She could let her run or jerk her back or stop her short. She could take the whole night to enjoy the pleasures of the chase, the excitement of stealth, her own fleet, buoyant body that did not yield to hunger, cold, or nerves. After such a night the girl would be well broken. She would live within the rules and by the timetable, speak softly, and never play with older boys.

For some time Marit had felt her pace grow faster. She smiled in the dark to think that revenge had put wings on her heels. Now the darkness began to lift, troubling her vision for a moment, but not her footing. The trees had thinned out, admitting some rays from the moon. In the paler light, she could see that the woods ran downhill. Gravity, not revenge, had quickened her motion.

The girl up ahead had risen to her feet. She was leaning backward, her chin tucked into her chest, one arm in front of her face to protect her eyes. On such steep terrain she could not control her balance. She stumbled headlong, breaking her fall against one tree, losing her grip and pitching forward against another. She was on a runaway course, unreined, flung from trunk to trunk, playing blindman's buff with giants in a waking nightmare.

The girl was hurtling downward. She was losing her. Marit was running with extra care, to save her neck. The downgrade grew sharper, inclining to perpendicular. Marit lengthened her stride; she was still several trees behind her. The girl's head bobbled as if it were working loose. From her mouth came a high trilling scream, a sound heard sometimes in extremes of pleasure. Her head jiggled and turned, making almost a full rotation. Marit saw her face. It was wizened with fear, old and doomed, screaming words or parts of words, louder and louder on the final plunge, five zigzag falls before Marit could hear that she had cried for help.

The woods cleared, giving way to a narrow bank. There were no trees here to curb Aimée's last fall—into Yoke Pond, fed by springs and deep as a mine. Openmouthed and unwarned, she swallowed two lungsful of water. She sank as if she were weighted down with stones.

Marit heard the splash as she fell. The unexpected sound, as sharp as gunfire, made her remember the rockbound pool beyond the trees, a pond that she had only seen from the other side, the side that lay within the boundaries of her land. As she moved down toward the bank, she hesitated, waiting to hear more splashing in the water, or coughing, or another cry for help, the sounds of the blind girl flailing on the surface. It was such a little pond, seven strokes at most to swim its entire length, surrounded by rocks that offered a ready handhold.

At the edge of the clearing she slid on matted leaves, and braced herself against a leaning birch. She saw the water churning into ripples. Wavelets beat against the rocks

and drenched the bank. There seemed to be no cause for the
disturbance, no shape upon the surface or below. She had
lost sight of the girl for no more than ninety seconds.
Drowning takes longer, even in deep water. The girl had
escaped and climbed out on dry land. She had groped her
way up the bank and found her footing. She would blunder
into the open where Marit could spot her. Marit would lift
her up and take her by the hand, and guide her through the
forest back to Meyerling. When they had reached the lawn,
she would point her toward the mansion, waiting to see that
she did not stray again.

It was taking the girl too long to show herself. Marit
leaned on the birch to brace her trembling limbs. The pond
was ebbing into glassy calm. If the girl was safe, she must
be very near, near enough to hear Marit's faulty, ragged
breathing, near enough to have sighted Marit's own position, with the extra senses given to the blind. She was hiding
from Marit, or waiting to make a move. Her feelings for her
pursuer would not be friendly. She would take her revenge
in kind, close in on Marit by inches, and hunt her down.

All at once the night was filled with warning sounds, a
chittering on her right, a thud, like an object falling, from
behind. A swish, repeated twice, the sound of a branch or
stick swung through the air. She heard a clatter and a hollow plop. A stone rolled over rock into the pond. There was
movement at the far side of the water, two young trees
swaying when there was no wind.

Marit felt her scalp rise and her chest grow cold. A
dark shape filled the breach between the saplings, looming
as she watched, then shrinking out of sight. On feet that felt
as soft as dampened putty, she edged away, still clinging to
the birch.

A cloud passed over, blocking out the moon, plunging the forest into sudden darkness. Another light went off, in Marit's mind. A grouse whirred out of hiding, just uphill. She heard the drumming louder than a siren. She screamed and ran, like running through a quagmire, where every footstep seemed to pull her down.

When the sun came up in the morning, the surface of the water reflected the first red rays. The pond was empty, except for dragonflies fishing. The grass on the bank had sprung back tall and wavy, erasing the human footprints that had crushed it flat.

NINE

D u r i n g the summer camp season, all of Meyerling rises, or is wrenched from sleep, at 6:30 a.m., to the sound of Daisy Fellowes singing "Good Morning, Mr. Yellowbird," piped at top volume over speakers that were set on every floor and hall. Miss Fellowes had been singing reveille for so many years that it had become a camp tradition, and had given rise to another accepted practice, sabotaging the loudspeakers.

This Tuesday morning, August 12th, black-haired Miss Muskie climbed on a chair to untie the down parka that she had wrapped around the speaker on the older girls' hall the night before. One parka had failed; but three would not have done the job. The boys' wing was still asleep. Conrad, the new swimming instructor, had disconnected the lead wires; he had been told that it would be unsporting if he cut them. Other methods had been tried, under the mistaken notion that plugging up the cloth face of the speakers would lower the volume of Daisy Fellowes' gravelly voice. Earlier in the season, John had stood on Wyeth's shoulders, chewing a mouthful of bubble gum, and popped large pink bubbles against the nylon mesh. The episodes of the rubber cement and the Spackle, three years before, had resulted in the firing of a woodworking counselor who was barely older than the boys on his floor. No one knew when Dufton and Fellowes might crack down on the speaker pranks; they seemed to play it entirely by whim.

Out of forty campers at Meyerling, ten boys were missing at breakfast, not to mention Conrad. Such a striking number of truants concealed the absence of a lone girl camper, a girl who had been late in the mornings in any case, and who complained that at home she always had breakfast in bed. Boys began straggling downstairs, singly or in twos, tripping on their shoelaces, shirttails slopping over their belts in back, looking hangdog and pleased with themselves. Each time a new group arrived, Miss Fellowes walked around all four tables, slapping the tops of heads and counting out loud. After seven headcounts she called the roll. Then she ordered Gabriel to take attendance again to verify her tally.

Aimée Dupuis was not accounted for. Fellowes ordered Muskie to get her up. Looking as remorseful as if he had been one of the latecomers himself, Henry Dufton announced that the whole camp would be benched for the day and confined to their rooms. The children began growling and buzzing. Mr. Dufton relented, as he always did at the first sign of protest. Miss Fellowes intervened and restated the punishment. Twenty cords of wood had been cut for the winter and lay stacked at the bottom of the meadow near the tennis courts. The campers would take the logs, as much as frail or husky arms could carry at one time, the quarter of a mile from the meadow to the woodshed, until every log was neatly piled inside: "Like busy ants, children, working for the good of the colony!"

Miss Fellowes was explaining how the pyramids had been built, evoking long files of black Egyptians hauling stones; Wyeth was squashing pieces of bread and stuffing them in his ears; and Nannie was sinking slowly beneath the mahogany horizon of the table when Miss Muskie came back, flapping like a hen, too distressed to take Miss Fellowes aside, and blurted out for all the children to hear that Aimée was missing. Her bed was made up and her toothbrush was dry. Her clothes were in the closet and the drawers. The maids and the cook had not seen her; neither had the groom nor the handyman. The gardener had found a wadded handkerchief near the rhododendrons with the initial "A" worked on one corner. Miss Muskie stretched the handkerchief out in front of her, the way bridal sheets are displayed after a peasant wedding.

"She was waylaid." Miss Muskie broke down. "Waylaid and raped!"

The dining room broke into an uproar, composed of one part shock and two parts glee. Those children who did not know what "rape" meant were clued in by those who did. Preston was wrestling Nannie to the floor. She had eclipsed herself under the table and pinched the first flesh she made contact with, Preston's calf. Several chairs toppled backward. One of them hit Preston, who collapsed over Nannie, pinning her down with his full weight. This looked remarkably like the fate of poor lost Aimée. Miss Muskie began to scream. Mr. Dufton was tapping his water glass with a knife blade. Gabriel cocked his head at Conrad in the direction of the terrace doors. They converged on Miss Muskie from opposite sides of the room. Too late. She had had her say: she had seen a hatted man in the lemon garden, and a bearded youth on one of the floors, who claimed to be a glazier. She had reported both men, but no one had paid attention.

The cook entered the fray. She would like to know who had stolen her boning knife; moreover, what were those muddy streaks on her clean kitchen floor? And with the price of Scottish oatmeal, she would not take the blame if most of it went to waste.

John took this as a signal to flip blobs of cereal, stone cold in his bowl, off the end of his spoon. Some fell on the floor; some landed in the hair of his tablemates, who were forced to fight back with milk, eggshells, toast rinds, salt-cellars, tea bags, and jam. Six boarding counselors, one of whom was beside herself, were not enough to quell thirty-nine storming children. There would have been seven counselors on hand, but Miss Fellowes had left the scene, pressing her palms to her temples, a flighty gesture that was most unlike her.

The fire alarm cut through the room, a noise that can paralyze the nervous system. Frozen in place for several moments, the children were docile when Fellowes reap-peared and called them into drill formation. In a real fire drill they would have been led down the driveway to the gates. For this diversionary exercise she marched them out to the back lawn, where she left Conrad to run them through an hour of tiring calisthenics.

No one but Gabriel wanted to call the Sheriff. Mr. Dufton wavered. Miss Muskie was not consulted. She was lying on a cot in the infirmary with a wet tea bag covering each of her swollen eyes. The discussion raged around the issue of Muskie's credibility. Muskie was both coquettish and fearful, a textbook hysteric. She saw rapists and perverts behind every bush. She wedged a chair under her bedroom door, and set empty bottles on her third-story windowsill which would crash to the floor and alert her in case of a break-in. When she was relieved of after-dinner switchboard duty, the number of breathers, and worse, had dwindled to zero. She hoarded food in her room, which attracted mice.

This sort of free-for-all character assassination, known in boarding schools—both blind and sighted—as a lemon-squeeze, usually takes place in the presence of the person who is under fire. Gabriel raised his voice and objected that Muskie was not on hand to defend herself. Fellowes remembered that Muskie had allowed Nannie to sleep with the school cat. Gabriel pushed the issue of Aimée's disappearance front and center. Mr. Dufton appealed to the group. Her family were lovely people, related to the Bourbons. Miss Withus spoke up; she had been there a week, running the arts and crafts program. She believed in attitude probation for girls like Aimée. Aimée's nightgowns had matching peignoirs. She had brought her own linen sheets. She was insolent in Braille tutorial. She moved her lips during morning meditation. At some point between the nightgowns and the tutorial, Gabriel went to the switchboard in the hallway and dialed Sheriff Stoeber.

Three people saw Marit's white convertible Buick parked near the main gates of Meyerling: the Sheriff, answering the emergency call which had come through on his van radio; Gabriel, pacing up and down the road, waiting for the police; and Lola, who was driving to Niles on an errand for Mrs. Gilliam. The white convertible was parked at Yelping Hill overlook, a rest area equipped with a coin-operated telescope. The telescope was out of order, and trees had grown back so high that they blocked the view. If the Buick had been set neatly between the lines painted on the asphalt, it would have attracted no notice. It had been backed in at an angle, across four marked spaces. The top was raised part of the way, with a wide gap between the canvas and the window frame. The door on the driver's side was ajar. The car looked abandoned.

Lola was carrying two lengths of silk from a wrong dye lot to return to Sarah Rippey. When she arrived, Rippey's Yard Goods looked like the scene of a year-end sale. As she pushed her way through the crowd roosting and squawking on the porch, she could see that all the customers were outside. Only Sarah herself was inside the shop, stationed by an open window. Lola put her package on the counter and turned to Sarah, who waved a hand to silence her. Lola went over to the window.

The center of the commotion seemed to be Eleanor Stoeber. Eleanor had all her teeth in her head and was beaming satisfied smiles, like a person receiving congratulations. Lola wondered what happy news could collect such a swarm, all women except for a few male teenage hangabouts. If Anna Weebs had left the post office unattended, it must be the birth of a grandchild or a transfer for the Sheriff. Anna's face was grim; but then, she did not have a hopeful temperament. She had an arm around her daughter's shoulders; Rosie squirmed in her grasp. Everyone was talking at once. Lola's view was a pool of open mouths and clacking teeth. She made another attempt to lure Sarah back to business. She was leaning toward Sarah to shout her request when one word floated up from the din and hung over the crowd like a caption in a comic-strip balloon. The word was "kidnapped."

With a verbal clue to guide her, Lola's brain came to the aid of her ears. After that, she could piece things together. A girl from the blind school was missing. The girl was rich. All those children were rich. That fancy school paid taxes to sneeze at, and they had made no exception to help out a local boy. Tick Brower, blinded cleaning his gun, had to go to the state school in Griggsville, that ugly place that was part of the mental hospital. The Sheriff had warned the principal at Meyerling that he was asking for trouble, with no guards and no fences, not even a pair of watchdogs. Eleanor did not like to say that the Sheriff had powers, but something had told him to put on an extra car the night three North Adams boys tried to hold up the filling station. When her husband said something was wrong up at the Deym estate, she would be the last person to doubt him. The Deym girl might be free with her money, like her Russian parents, but she kept apart. The father was some kind of royalty, no proof against dying with his mind gone. The Sheriff said the daughter had had her own way once too often, making her place into a private zoo—the same as having a prison right in town, with convicts getting loose and harming the neighbors.

Lola could no more have walked through the group on the porch again than work a hive on a cloudy day without a bee veil. Sarah was carried away, and sniping along with the rest of them. Lola let herself out by the rear door, which was hidden behind a paneled screen. As she slipped back to her car, the voices seemed to grow louder.

This was the part of life in a village that made her sweat, all these women thinking with one mind, gulping down bigger and bigger chunks of alarm and figment, competing like entrants in a pie-eating contest, except that an excess of rumor did not make them sick, but greedier.

There was no proof that a child had been kidnapped, only the Sheriff's intuition. The Sheriff had intuitions in the way carcasses have maggots, from moldering too long in a backwater. The Sheriff went to police seminars in Boston to make his work lively, since race riots, espionage and bookmaking did not flourish in Niles. His conversation was a perpetual bid for omniscience, a habit that he had passed on to his bride. Lola recalled the little panic of '56, when the Stoebers had predicted a national shortage of white candles. Stores laid in by Mrs. Gilliam alone would have been enough to start one.

But the Stoebers' self-importance was not so humorous when it threatened Marit, whose showy car had been dumped near Meyerling, for no good reason, before nine in the morning; who was flaunting the law in secret, harboring wolves like marked cards in a crooked poker game; whose natural cunning was being sapped by a priggish schoolteacher named Gabriel Frankman. There had been swells of talk about the animal sanctuary from the beginning, talk about drafting a petition, about taking Marit to court, about sending in an inspector from the village—namely, the Sheriff. Like a deceived wife, Marit had heard little of these murmurs, even at their loudest. Lola never played the role of the well-intentioned friend, bringing loose talk back to Marit for her own good. Villages were fickle toward the objects of their malice; in another year they would brag about their wildlife preserve and take the credit for it.

At ten o'clock, Mrs. Gilliam expected Lola at her bedside to go over the mail and menus and to plan her wardrobe. After breakfast, there would be a session with the auction notices and the fall bulb catalogues. Then, Lola had promised to bake her mother's Benne wafers for a formal tea. Between three and four Mrs. Gilliam took a nap, for the purpose of wearing her frown patches. During that free hour, Lola could try to get through to Marit, if only to relieve her fretful imagination, which kept flashing pictures of Marit's white car still unclaimed by nightfall.

The rays of the sun woke Marit from a stony sleep. For a moment she thought she had gone to bed with all her clothes on, rank garments which made her nostrils wrinkle at their smell. She was very hot, as if there were too many blankets covering her. Her head ached and she resisted opening her eyes. She reached out to fumble for the clock on the bedside table, but her arm fell instead on a solid mass of fur. She raised her head and saw that Nikolai was pressed up against her. She saw a section of wire mesh fence and two metal bowls. She was not upstairs on the little cot in her childhood bedroom; she was lying on the concrete pavement inside Nikolai's pen.

Marit buried her face in Nikolai's coat and held him too tightly. He grunted in protest and struggled to roll away.

As long as she held him she would not have to think or remember; she could pretend that she did not know the reason
for the leaden weight around her heart. The dog, who was
hungry and whining, broke out of her grasp, and began to
push at his empty food dish with his nose. Marit got up on
her knees and put her arms around his neck.

"Lola will take you," she said, but Nikolai shook her
off, "Lola will keep you if I can't."

Lola would take Nikolai and give him a loving home.
She could not keep the wolves or the lynx or the two black
bears. No one could keep them. Marit doubled over under
the force of returning memory. She struck at her head with
her fists, but the blows felt too light. She ran out of the pen
and dashed her head against the side of the house. Pain
blinded and staggered her, but not long enough; she could
not numb her brain, or halt the deadly logic of her thoughts.
She had left her white car on the road. Her car would condemn her. The Sheriff would come to get her and put her
away. He would profit by her absence to enter the sanctuary
and butcher the animals.

Marit paced up and down the terrace, taking quick
frantic steps, almost skipping, back and forth across the
length of the terrace, until she heard the malamute howling.
Then she stopped in her tracks with a jerk, like a motor run
down. She straightened her back and dropped her shoulders.
She found her center of balance and placed her full weight
on her feet. Now she was grounded, and her mind was free
to calculate and plan. There were many small tasks to perform and time was against her: enough food for Nikolai; a
letter to Lola; a knapsack to pack. . . . She stepped forward
and looked up at her house. The gutters on the second story

were choked by wisteria. She might not be back to give her
gardener the order to tear the vine down.

If diagramed in time of emergency, Gabriel's mind would be
layered like the earth's crust, with desire buried under suc-
cessive levels of duty. If he relaxed his will, these layers
might shift or splinter, under the impact, for example, of the
sight of Marit's car forced on his vision at a moment when
he needed his attention whole. To bring himself back to the
crisis at hand, he stopped pacing, turned his back to the car,
and performed a simple exercise: he repeated the phrase "I
am empty" until he was once more quiet and alert. Twenty-
five repetitions restored him. If he had a divided mind, he
could not be useful. He had no right to private thoughts
until the girl was found.

He accused himself of indifference in the face of need.
For the last four days, the girl had been begging for help,
coming to his room each night after curfew, her feet naked,
the straps of her thin nightdress hanging off her shoulders,
so harassed and unhappy that she had not taken time to
put on a robe. Sunday night the straps had slipped down to
bare one of her breasts. This neglect of her person should
have warned him that her nightmares were a sign of a
deeper problem. Every one of his actions had been per-
functory. He gave her two aspirins with a cup of water. He
tucked a blanket around her, since the night air was cool
and had made her nipples hard. He sat with her for a long
time, holding her hand, letting her talk herself out. He listened to what she said, but with half a mind. He heard
enough to think that her trouble was beyond his scope, a
motherless girl whose father took her into his bed when bad

dreams woke her, who could only sleep through the night if the father stayed by her until her eyes closed.

While she talked the girl had pressed his hand, as if she sensed that he was thinking other thoughts, none to be proud of, the reasons that an old friend had given him for leaving medicine. Dick Ardery did not like to work with patients: "They don't want you to have a life, Gabriel; why do you think they call you 'my doctor'? They hate you to eat or take a break or treat someone else." This urgent Dupuis girl did not want Gabriel to have a life. She wanted a robot helper that was never tired, or sick in love, or disillusioned with Meyerling; that would not notice the tyranny of sick people, or the pride with which they narrated their symptoms. His conscience worked out an equation that balanced perfectly: he had nurtured resentment toward her/she had run away. If she found herself in danger, it was on his head.

A black patrol wagon rounded the curve with a squeal of rubber. The Sheriff was grinning and waving as if he were the lead car in a parade. Gabriel thumbed him down and rode with him back to the house.

New England is full of ponds that are used as swimming holes. On a very blue day their surface reflects the sky, but their ordinary color is brown or yellowish-brown, from the quantity of leaves that drop into them autumn after autumn. People who have never swum in the ocean or who live far from lakes do not mind sharing a pond with tadpoles, water beetles, green scum, turtles, and catfish. They do not imagine the feelers of the catfish brushing their legs, or the slimy, whiskery plants that grow on the bottom. These swimmers hold their noses, and sink down to test the depth.

When their toes reach the soft, sucking mud, they do not shoot to the surface in horror and paddle for shore. Instead they drift to the top and laze on their backs for hours, swatting off darning needles.

No one swims in Yoke Pond, because it is lost in the woods. It is as deep as a quarry and one side is scooped out of rock. Layers of rock jut under the water, which makes diving perilous. Since the water is cold, it breeds no green scum and no catfish. The color of the water is black; steely-gray in winter when the trees have lost their leaves.

Yoke Pond is the home of turtles, some as small as the kind that children keep in boxes, some that are six or seven inches across the carapace. Their shells are decorated with concentric hexagons, like coffering on a vault, or with a random pattern of white spots. These gentle swimmers, half deaf and voiceless, live and multiply undisturbed by man, though birds and raccoons make raids on their helpless young. Turtles have no teeth, but their jaws have sawlike edges. They tear their food into pieces and swallow the pieces whole. They will eat leaves, shoots, and berries, but they like meat better, snails, tadpoles, flies and gnats, and little fish.

Sometimes, as it had done this summer, the turtle colony outgrows its supply of food. When the girl Aimée fell into the pond, the turtles were hungry. The girl plunged to a considerable depth, choking on water. On the way up she struck her head on a jut of rock lying under the surface. The broad slab pinned her there until she had finished drowning. Her fall drove the turtles away, onto land or out to the far side of the pond. After the water had settled, they came back to explore and smell, and stayed to feed.

Under water, human flesh becomes loose and softened,

making it more pliable to a turtle's jaws. Even then her skin was denser than the meat of their normal prey, so they had to work for their meal, massing in squadrons at the parts of the body that were unclothed, spelling each other, unit after unit, in an orderly lineup. Hundreds of turtles, grinding and eating, stirred the water, making currents that moved the body from side to side, pushing it over a stretch of time toward the end of the jut, where it floated free to the top.

For all their numbers and exertions the turtles did minor damage. There was plenty left of Aimée when the search party found her later, enough to make a positive identification by the clothes she wore, if not by her face or the pads of her fingers and toes. She was riddled with little holes, as if she had been used as a target by a marksman firing an air gun. Skeeter Brower got sick when he saw her, and he was a big, rough man who could skin a rabbit in one motion and who butchered his own venison.

Brower, Gabriel, and the Sheriff made up the search party, along with Conrad, Bill Weebs, and Deputy Crocker, whose business was artesian wells, with a sideline in taxidermy. Weebs was out of work for the second time that year. Anna had turned him out of the bedroom into the cellar, where he slept on a cot in the workroom, hanging his clothes on pegs and pairs of nails, over the saws and wrenches. The Deputy enlisted Weebs for the price of a six-pack, since Anna kept him on dole, a child's allowance that did not cover tobacco and beer.

Bill Weebs got some of his juice back fanning out through the woods with a black leather gun belt strapped around his waist, hearing his own voice crackle over the walkie-talkie. He was the right man for the job. Besides himself, Brower was the only able woodsman. The blond kid, Conrad, had an athletic build, but he was afraid of catching his feet and walked with his head down. The runty dark one, some kind of teacher, wasn't good for much; the Sheriff had offered him a pistol and he refused to take it. Stoeber and Crocker were out of shape; they spent the whole day at a desk or in a car.

Weebs had his big moment shortly after noon. On the level ground inside the virgin forest, his hawk eye detected a brown sandal, still buckled, with the bottom peeling away from the inner sole. It lay propped at the base of a maple with the toe pointing upward, as if its owner had climbed the tree at right angles, like a nuthatch or a creeper. The sandal was passed from hand to hand squeamishly, dangled by the ankle strap. The leather was damp. The sandal was an odd size, big for a young girl, but small for any rapist or kidnapper. The stitching had been done by hand, according to Conrad. There was a long debate about whether it had been wrenched off the foot of the victim, removed voluntarily, or had slipped off during a chase. The mute, ungainly article derailed the search, until Gabriel proposed that sandals are worn in pairs.

Gabriel's statement put the Sheriff in mind of his favorite grievance. The County expected him to operate on a shoestring. He had filed an order for a copying machine and they gave him enough to buy a secondhand typewriter. He had asked for a police dog and they sent him a handsome fellow that had failed the training. One good Doberman— not Dr. Whitbeck's, who was a one-man dog—would have saved them all this aimless tramping, with nothing to show for it but a mateless sandal.

Weebs was geared to take this remark as a personal insult when Brower put his hand by his ear and hissed to shut him up. Each man heard what he heard, a naked drawn-out howl, repeated at a higher pitch, up the scale, then down, a dirge sung in parts, a wintry, midnight call, untimely in the noonday sun and the summer heat. The mournful sound continued in full chorus, until separate voices trailed off to a whine, or a breaking sigh. None of the men could place the sound or name the singer—owl, loon, beast or maddened human, or nothing living.

The downhill stretch of forest began abruptly, as if the land had slid away in a glacial age. The search party formed a unit and worked in silence, heading in the direction of the cries. They filed behind the Sheriff, moving from tree to tree, using the trees to cover their approach, walking on the balls of their feet with their weapons drawn.

The search had started as an outing, a hike for sport and pleasure, a practice maneuver like war games, rigged to provide excitement but not suspense. The Sheriff's hopes of kidnappers had been giddy and short. Every man figured that the excursion would probably end back at the school, drinking coffee in the servants' dining room, while a shivering runaway, who had roamed about as far as the hayloft in the stable, was being put to bed upstairs in the infirmary and given a dose of cough syrup for good measure. The howling from the bottom of the slope tolled other images, ambush and slaughter. They no longer expected to find the girl alive. Whatever had taken her life was also a threat to them.

On the steepest part of the descent they saw a flare, a brief, unsteady light that flashed at intervals, like signals on a landing field at night. They could not yet see Yoke Pond, or the rays of sunlight glaring off the water, shining through the trees whenever the wind waved the topmost branches.

They were ready to attack. The Sheriff motioned them to pick up their pace. He made them take the final incline at a run. They were more fortunate than the lost dead girl. When the trees stopped, three feet from the pond, they could see the water and rear back to keep from falling.

At their feet, wedged between rocks, floated the body, covered with little tears, like rotten cloth, face up, but lacking eyelids, lips, and cheeks. Brower felt his stomach heave and turned his back. Conrad swayed forward and Gabriel caught him going down. Weebs, Stoeber, and Crocker moved in to study the tattered remnants.

Across the pond an honor guard stood watching, three wolves—the old one, Swan, and the lame wolf, George, flanked by the young male, Killik, who pawed the ground to urge the others to retreat, snarling in the back of his throat at the sight of men.

Weebs had a slow and mulish brain, but his hands were quick. He raised his gun and fired. The wolves were faster. Four shots raised clods of earth on the farther bank. The fifth hit rock and skipped back in the water. Gunfire covered the sound of trampled brush, but the men saw a streak of gray below the bank, running into sparser woods beyond their range.

The Sheriff had lost interest in the victim. Gabriel dragged her out of the water by her clothes, gripping the waistband of her shorts and the front of her jersey. He laid her on the bank and kneeled beside her. He took her cold hands in his, and forced himself to hold them until the impulse to recoil had passed. In order to carry her back to the school, they would have to knot their shirts to make a litter.

There would not be enough shirts to hold the sodden weight and have one left over to cover her and hide her.

The Sheriff was smiling and nodding. He had been waiting for an event to tip his hand.

"That's the Deym place," he said, pointing down the bank. "We'll have to go in after them."

Wolves are frauds, and the language abets them. A lewd man is a wolf; greedy feeders have wolfish appetites. The wolf at the door is poverty, cold and starvation. Liars cry wolf; lone wolves are unsocial and ominous. A famous murderer was nicknamed the Wolf of Buxton. The popular image of a wolf is a false face painted with bloody fangs and pointed ears, and a ring of black outlining its slanted eyes.

There is no one around to puncture their bad reputation, although a man in Colorado once taught some wolves to sing, and another man claimed that they subsisted entirely on mice. Marit Deym never tried to defend them. She locked them up and appointed herself their guardian. An optimistic person might have handed out leaflets explaining the place of the wolf in the ecological scheme, or the ability of wolves to form emotional attachments. Marit knew that her neighbors preferred the homicidal image, the way the people of Salem preferred to believe in witches. The Sheriff did not look beyond the wolves for the cause of the lost girl's death, or stop to reason that her wounds were much too small to have been cut by teeth, that wolves do not like to swim, that they will never attack a man unless they are rabid. The wolves played into the Sheriff's hands: they were found at the scene of the crime; they belonged to someone who had treated him like a servant; they were molting, be-

cause it was summer, and their ragged fur had made them
look ugly and vicious.

The next morning, Wednesday, a workday, the village of
Niles declared a celebration, or so it would have seemed to a
traveler passing through, who could not otherwise explain
the cars lining up on the main street, and the people milling
in among the cars, pounding a drumbeat on the hoods,
reaching in and leaning on horns (after a friendly tussle
with the drivers), loading cases of beer into the trunks. The
cars sat with their engines idling, as if they were ready to go
and waiting for a signal. Some of the women were carrying
baskets packed with food, and the general store was doing
good business in cold cuts and rolls. There were no flags
flying and no bunting draped on the storefronts. There was
no one rigged out in knee britches, or shouldering muskets,
so it was not a national holiday or the town centennial.

The traveler, waiting in his car for the crowd to let him
through, might have wondered why a man dressed in the
blues and boots of a state trooper was passing out shells, by
handfuls or in square green boxes. None of the men, old or
young, was carrying shotguns, and the legal hunting season
was months away. Looking closer, since his wait was going
to be a long one, the traveler would be bound to notice that
almost every man did hold some object in his hand—an axe,
a cane, a jack handle, a crowbar, or, in some cases, thick
dowels or heavy sticks. Two boys had finished coiling a
length of rope. On the porch of the general store, a woman
in a dirty butcher's apron waved at someone in the street
and held up a metal ring in both hands. It was a spring trap,
the kind with close-set, jagged teeth.

* * *

Lola knew that Marit had contempt for the telephone. It was nothing to her to let the bell ring if she did not want to hear a voice from the outside world. Marit did not scowl at the instrument or take if off the hook; she ignored it and went on working or reading. Lola always answered her phone, but she waited two rings so that the caller would not think she was overeager. Lola wrote thank-you notes the morning after a party; she had been known to send a note after a half-hour visit. The difference in their styles caused many quarrels. Lola had begged Marit for a private code: ring once, hang up, then ring again. Lola found the idea that Marit would not make an exception in her case more provoking than the fact that she could not reach her. It did not do to go knock on her door when she was not answering. Marit felt no more obligation to doorbells than she did to telephones.

Marit's rules of privacy might apply in normal times; they did not hold when a student at Meyerling had been bitten to death and the whole town was raving that a pack of wolves had killed her. Mrs. Gilliam's black cook, Vyselle, got the news from the delivery market in East Niles when she called in the day's order for groceries. Lola left a message for Mrs. G., who was still asleep, and drove off without eating breakfast or doing her face.

The road was clear, and the speedometer kept creeping up to seventy. Lola's mind was not on the road. When she was not trying to suppress a connection between Marit's silence, her abandoned car, and the death of the student, she was counting the entrances to Marit's house, front door, kitchen door, side door, cellar, conservatory. There were seventeen windows on the ground floor, probably locked up tight because Marit checked the fastenings more than once before retiring at night. If the doors were locked, Lola was ready to smash a window.

It was no surprise that the circular driveway in front of the Deym house was empty; but the blinds on every window had been pulled down, and the local newspaper was lying on the bottom step. Lola raised the brass knocker, a rampant eagle, then caught it before it could fall and strike the plate. She went around by the service path to the back of the house. A curtain had been drawn inside the window in the kitchen door. She crossed the terrace to look through the glassed-in conservatory, passing blinded and curtained windows on all four stories. She heard voices rising and falling and moved toward the house, until she realized that the sound came from behind her, from the meadow below the acre of green lawn, the uncut field that bordered the main gate to the sanctuary.

The body, no longer referred to by name, was lying under a tarpaulin in the Bishop's wine cellar, which was the coolest room in the mansion, waiting to be taken away by the Dupuis family and their Hartford funeral people. Prompted by Miss Fellowes, Henry Dufton had decided to disband the summer camp session. He and Miss Fellowes had locked themselves in the library to call the parents, since they had also resolved that the children must not be told why they were going home early. The children knew perfectly well that their schoolmate was dead, and would tell their fathers and mothers that Mr. Dufton had whipped her to death for staying out all night. There would be a large number of withdrawals for the fall term, and dwindling applications, owing to word of mouth, for several years.

Gabriel prided himself on his reflexes in a crisis. He took charge when a fellow diner in a restaurant keeled over at a nearby table, or when an old woman loaded with shopping bags fell down on an icy street. The crisis at Meyerling had passed him by. He might have found relief in mindless chores, but the other counselors had hogged all the duties, packing the children's suitcases, distracting the cook, standing guard by the wine cellar. No one pressed him into service. His leadership qualities did not seem to be required.

He was not needed at Meyerling; but he would be needed at the Deym place, where another crisis was brewing, if he had heard right. His appetite for emergency was depleted. He tried to summon up his love for Marit, as a goad. His feelings failed him, as his stamina had failed him. He set out along the main road to the Deym house, choosing the longest and the hardest route.

Gabriel toiled three miles along the highway on foot, refusing rides from a baker's truck and a youth on a motorcycle. The asphalt surface had softened in the heat, and burned through the rubber soles of his canvas shoes. The glare was intense; black dots swarmed in front of his eyes like avenging gnats. A case of migraine and blisters were fit companions in his state, since this was the head that had reasoned that Aimée must practice walking by herself, and these were the feet that had refused to guide her from the chapel to the mansion. If wolves had killed her, as the Sheriff contended, then Gabriel had fed her to the wolves; if she drowned before the animals had found her, then Gabriel had held her under water.

He turned down the rutted road that led into the woods, the same woods he had hiked through in better days, when he had only one death on his conscience. The woods were shady and still, but alive with insects. Soon Gabriel's arms were covered with swellings, which he would not scratch. Biting creatures hummed around his ears; he never raised a hand to brush them off. The stinging flies that dogged him were more merciful than his thoughts.

Marit would be faced by the Sheriff and his posse, demanding the expulsion of the wolves. It was his duty to stand by her and to give her what support he could, even though her feeling for the wolves repelled him, since they had played a part in taking a human life. Marit did not share his reverence for life; no man and woman should mate without shared values.

The road came out at the top of a high sloping meadow. The meadow grass was mashed down by tire tracks, which crisscrossed the field all the way to the sanctuary gates. Through the glare, which was as white and dense as mist, Gabriel saw a horde of people by the gates, a horde of colored specks forming and re-forming, and larger shapes reflecting the sunlight, which must be cars and trucks, brought to a stop, not parked, all over the bottom of the meadow. Masses of clouds were hanging in the sky that would later bring rain.

Gabriel stretched his neck in the heat, watching the cloud banks melding and changing, and the menagerie of figures formed by clouds: the ostrich, the dragon, and the bull, and the lion with its head resting on its paws. From this high place he could see two counties, one of them in a neighboring state, and the purplish crest of Greylock, which passed for a mountain among the Berkshire Hills. Gravity inclined him downward; but he did not hurry. For an instant he imagined retreating or deserting. He had no taste for crowds or angry litigation. A hawk soared overhead, riding the air currents, barking and scanning the ground for mice and grasshoppers. Gabriel felt his chest lift along with the hawk, but he stayed on the land, short and earthbound.

As he walked where gravity pushed him, bearing down on his heels, he began to hear the noise from the crowd, a carnival sound, high-pitched and excited, like bursts of laughter and the exchange of taunts and dares. His vision, weakened by the sun, was slowly clearing, enough to make out some holiday sights: a group of women unfolding a checkered cloth, a little boy pulling a toy wagon, a girl releasing a white balloon, which floated up and out of her reach, higher and higher, until it sailed over the cyclone fence. Gabriel wondered if Marit had opened the meadow to the villagers, as she did, from time to time, for the campers at Meyerling. The cluster of people at the gate must be waiting for her to bring the keys. Perhaps she was going to take them on a guided tour of the sanctuary, a shrewd plan which would defuse any panic that the Sheriff had been spreading. Gabriel glanced back up the slope at her house and the low stone railing surrounding the terrace. Someone was moving across the terrace, coming down the outside staircase at a run. It was a woman, but she was blonde and wore a skirt.

Gabriel was close enough to name some figures at the gate, Skeeter and his old man, Norb; Bill Weebs, squatting at the outer edge; Frank Segalla, the Meyerling handyman, with a bandanna tied around his neck to catch the sweat. He saw the Sheriff's ten-gallon hat at the center of the group, but the Sheriff himself was dwarfed by taller bodies. Suddenly the crowd fell back. The hat and the man were hunched over the padlock, ramming a metal bar through the shackle of the lock and between the gateposts, leaning on the bar and forcing it sideways. The fence posts clashed, but the padlock held. Brower moved in with an axe, pushed the Sheriff aside, and struck the lock with the head of the axe. The lock sprung. The gate wavered open. The men roared and the women clapped.

Gabriel waited, but the crowd did not pour through the gate. They ran back through the field where the cars were scattered; they were going to drive into the sanctuary. There was no service road; the cars with low chassis would never make it. Gabriel tried to move, but his legs felt like stretched-out elastic. He saw rear doors pulled open and trunk lids snapped up so hard that they bounced on their hinges, threatening to slam closed on the legs or the heads of the men who were reaching inside. Gabriel had some force left in his arms. He raised a hand to wave, but the gesture was feeble. The men emerged from their cars. Gabriel shut his eyes. He did not see them loading the chambers of their deer rifles. By the time he could look again, they were inside the fence, keeping down and spreading out into the brush like commandos.

The body of Marit Deym lay where it fell. The bullet that had entered her chest would have passed between the eyes of the wolf whom she called Swan. The old wolf licked her face and pushed her with his nose to break her sleep. Two wolf pups tumbled over her feet, snuffling and growling and biting each other's paws. The young male, Killik, sat at rest, like a watchdog chained up. In the wide clearing where Marit had jumped from the top of the fence the Friday before, a ring of men, their guns on the ground, hung back in the shadows, which were deepening as the afternoon sun moved down the sky. The wolves had claimed Marit's body, taking precedence over any human kin.

It was never clear whose bullet had killed her, since no one came forward to contest the dubious honor. When the wolves strayed into the open, more than one man had taken aim and pressed the trigger. Marit had appeared from nowhere and jumped into the line of fire. Behind a laurel bush near her body, someone found a rolled-up blanket and a canvas bag, filled with cans of food, two sweaters, and a box of matches. Lola, who arrived too late, identified the clothes.

It was Lola who walked through the sentry pack of wolves, while the men looked down or turned their faces aside. She bent her cheek over Marit's mouth and felt no breath. The pulse was still when she pressed the vein at the base of her neck. There was a streak of dirt on Marit's forehead. Lola took out a handkerchief and rubbed the spot away. In death as in life, Marit's hair required attention. Lola combed it into order with her fingers.

Lola wanted to kiss Marit's cheek, which was not yet cold; but she would never have embarrassed her friend in front of such low company. She tried to read Marit's face, for a record of how she had lived her last few hours; but she could not see any traces of anguish or devastation. Marit's mouth was slightly open and her face wore a little frown, the puzzled expression of a sleeper who may be dreaming. For a second she was cross with Marit, and wanted to shake her, as if Marit was holding back and refusing to confide in order to tease her.

As she laid Marit's outspread arms along her body, Lola noticed the heavy ring she always wore, Vlado's ring, with a coat of arms engraved in onyx, a chevron between three towers, the towers in flames. Lola took the ring off and tried it on her hand. It fit the middle finger, where Marit had worn it. It was all Lola had left, except for a pair of Marit's socks, which she had borrowed on a rainy day and never returned.

Marit's ashes are locked in the Deym vault on the grounds of St. Stephen's in West Niles. Vlado and Luba were never Anglicans. They chose the church because Stephen was the patron saint of Hungary. Lola got into a mean tangle with the minister over Marit's burial. The Reverend Kip did not want the remains of a suicide in his churchyard. The rumor of suicide had been going around, spread by the townsfolk to ease a collective bad conscience. Lola argued lamely at first. Marit had owned a revolver, a delicate ladies' handgun of German make, but she had closed the house and gone to defend her wolves unarmed, unless the box of matches could be counted as a weapon. Then it occurred to Lola that the worthy Reverend could not read her mind. He did not guess that Marit could be charged with worse deeds than taking her life. Lola's arguments gained force and the Reverend knuckled under. She was proud of herself. She had settled her friend's affairs. Marit was her wolf, and she would guard her story from the knowledge of vicious men.

Gabriel left Meyerling one morning before the rising bell. He gave no notice and left no address. He never wrote for his wages or for his clothes, which may still be stored in a carton in the attic boxroom. His bed was unmade, but his desk had been cleared and emptied. For years he avoided the state of Massachusetts. He could not make himself tend two graves in the same Berkshire county.

A NOTE ABOUT THE AUTHOR

Ann Arensberg was born in Pittsburgh, Pennsylvania, was brought up in Havana, Cuba, and was educated at Radcliffe College and Harvard University. She has previously written two stories—"Art History" and "Group Sex"—both of which were selected for inclusion in O. Henry Awards collections. She lives with her husband in New York City and Salisbury, Connecticut.

A NOTE ON THE TYPE

This book was set on the Linotype in Janson, a recutting made direct from type cast from matrices long thought to have been made by the Dutchman Anton Janson, who was a practicing type founder in Leipzig during the years 1668–87. However, it has been conclusively demonstrated that these types are actually the work of Nicholas Kis (1650–1702), a Hungarian, who most probably learned his trade from the master Dutch type founder Dirk Voskens. The type is an excellent example of the influential and sturdy Dutch types that prevailed in England up to the time William Caslon developed his own in-comparable designs from them.

Composed by The Maryland Linotype Composition
Company, Inc., Baltimore, Maryland. Printed and bound
by The Haddon Craftsmen, Inc., Scranton, Pennsylvania.

Typography and binding design by Karolina Harris.